"The dam needs to be repaired," Charles said, "in more than one place."

"Can it be done cheaply?"

"I don't know," Charles replied. "I'm still thinking about that."

He looked around. They were meeting in the same low-rent saloon, but today they and the bartender were the only ones there.

"You better find a way to fix it, then," the man said. "That's what I'm paying you for."

"Well," Charles said, "if Clint Adams is here, that changes things."

"Why? How?"

"Because of my other profession. The one where I use my gun. That puts me right on a collision course with him."

"It doesn't have to."

"Yes, it does. He has one of the biggest reputations in the West with a gun. Maybe the biggest. You know what that means?"

"This is not the Wild West, Charles," the man said. "This is Pittsburgh. This is a civilized city."

"Is it? Have you read the papers lately? Three people have been killed in the past few days. How damn civilized is that?"

"Dash—"

"If I kill Clint Adams," Dash Charles said, "I won't need your money anymore."

DON'T MISS THESE
ALL-ACTION WESTERN SERIES
FROM THE BERKLEY PUBLISHING GROUP

THE GUNSMITH by J. R. Roberts

Clint Adams was a legend among lawmen, outlaws, and ladies. They called him . . . the Gunsmith.

LONGARM by Tabor Evans

The popular long-running series about Deputy U.S. Marshal Custis Long—his life, his loves, his fight for justice.

SLOCUM by Jake Logan

Today's longest-running action Western. John Slocum rides a deadly trail of hot blood and cold steel.

BUSHWHACKERS by B. J. Lanagan

An action-packed series by the creators of Longarm! The rousing adventures of the most brutal gang of cutthroats ever assembled—Quantrill's Raiders.

DIAMONDBACK by Guy Brewer

Dex Yancey is Diamondback, a Southern gentleman turned con man when his brother cheats him out of the family fortune. Ladies love him. Gamblers hate him. But nobody pulls one over on Dex . . .

WILDGUN by Jack Hanson

The blazing adventures of mountain man Will Barlow—from the creators of Longarm!

TEXAS TRACKER by Tom Calhoun

J.T. Law: the most relentless—and dangerous—manhunter in all Texas. Where sheriffs and posses fail, he's the best man to bring in the most vicious outlaws—for a price.

THE GUNSMITH
394
THE SOUTH FORK SHOWDOWN

J. R. ROBERTS

JOVE BOOKS, NEW YORK

THE BERKLEY PUBLISHING GROUP
Published by the Penguin Group
Penguin Group (USA) LLC
375 Hudson Street, New York, New York 10014

USA • Canada • UK • Ireland • Australia • New Zealand • India • South Africa • China

penguin.com

A Penguin Random House Company

THE SOUTH FORK SHOWDOWN

A Jove Book / published by arrangement with the author

For information, address: The Berkley Publishing Group,
a division of Penguin Group (USA) LLC,
375 Hudson Street, New York, New York 10014.

ISBN: 978-0-515-15497-9

PUBLISHING HISTORY
Jove mass-market edition / October 2014

PRINTED IN THE UNITED STATES OF AMERICA

10   9   8   7   6   5   4   3   2   1

Cover illustration by Sergio Giovine.

ONE

Pittsburgh lay sprawled out in front of Clint Adams as he regarded it from the saddle. He'd been to big cities like New York and Chicago, and other major cities like Denver and San Francisco. Pittsburgh had grown by leaps and bounds since the one and only other time he'd ever been there. A major city now with paved streets and multistory buildings. He knew there'd be elevators and telephones there. He didn't mind telephones, but he didn't like elevators. Not one bit.

"Let's go, big fella," he said to Eclipse, urging him into a canter. "Time to get down to business."

As he rode into the city, Clint saw the electric streetlights, the trolleys, and an occasional automobile. Pittsburgh was marching determinedly toward the twentieth century.

He reined in Eclipse in front of the Steel House Hotel and dismounted. He grabbed his carpetbag and rifle and entered the lobby.

The lobby had a high ceiling with a crystal chandelier, and was furnished with a half-dozen burgundy divans and just as many armchairs. The people milling about, entering and exiting the dining room, elevator, and staircases, were mostly well and expensively dressed.

He approached the front desk, and the clerk—also well dressed—eyed him dubiously, with one eyebrow arched.

"Yes?"

"I need a room."

"Indeed," the man said. "The rooms here are quite expensive, you know."

"Is that a fact?" Clint asked. "You want me to turn my pockets inside out for you?"

"Sir?"

"So you can count my money?"

"Sir," the man said, "that won't be necessary." The clerk turned the register to face him. "Just sign in and we'll see what we can do to find an appropriate room."

"Thank you."

Clint signed his name while the clerk made a show of trying to find him an "appropriate" room. Clint noticed he was looking along the bottom row of keys.

"Problem?" Clint asked, turning the register back around.

"Uh, no," the clerk said, "I'm just, uh . . ." He glanced at the register, then stopped and took a good long look.

"Adams?" he asked.

"That's right."

"Um, *the* Clint Adams?"

"I don't know of another one," Clint said. "Is that a problem?"

"Uh, no, sir, Mr. Adams," the clerk said. "No problem at all."

The clerk suddenly reached up and took a key from the top row. "Here we go."

"Thank you," Clint said, accepting the key.

"Would you like help with your bag, sir?"

"No," Clint said, "I've got it, thanks."

"Just let me know if there's anything at all the house can do to make your stay more pleasant, Mr. Adams."

"I'll do that."

Clint picked up his bag and rifle and walked to the stairs.

"Mr. Adams?"

He stopped, turned, and looked at the clerk.

"We have an elevator." The man pointed.

"What floor am I on?" Clint asked.

"The third."

"I can walk," Clint said, and started up the stairs.

After Clint Adams disappeared up the staircase, the clerk waved to one of the bellboys.

"Yes, Steve?"

"Jimmy," Steve Edison said to the bellboy, who was actually three years older than him, "find Mr. Frick."

"Sir?"

"Henry Frick," Steve said. "You know who he is?"

"Well, yeah, but . . . I ain't never talked to him."

"Well, find him and give him a message," Steve said.

"What's the message?"

Steve wrote it on a slip of paper and passed it to Jimmy.

"Just give him that."

"Okay."

"Do it now."

"I'm on duty—"

"No, Jimmy," Steve said. "I'll cover for you."

"Well, okay," Jimmy said dubiously.

"You won't lose any tips," Steve promised as Jimmy left.

TWO

In his room, Clint set the rifle down in a corner, dumped the bag on the big bed. The clerk had given him a large room. He had no way of knowing if it was one of the largest, though.

The hotel had indoor plumbing, which he'd seen a few times before. Water running into a basin from outside, a "water closet" with a pull chain flush toilet. The toilet had first appeared in England during the 1870s but, at the start of the 1880s, had begun appearing in the United States.

He washed up and made use of the toilet, then went back down to the lobby. The clerk straightened his back as he saw Clint approaching the desk.

"What's your name?" Clint asked.

"Steve, sir."

"Steve, how is the steak in your dining room?"

"The best in town."

"Are you supposed to say that, or is it actually the best in town?"

"Well . . . it's pretty good for a hotel dining room,"

Steve said. "But there are restaurants in town with better."

"Thanks for the honesty," Clint said. "I'll try it and let you know."

"Yes, sir," Steve said. "By the way, sir, you can sign your check in the dining room and then the meal will be charged to your room. You can pay for everything when you check out."

"Is that a fact?"

"Sir," the clerk said. "It's for your convenience."

"Well, thanks," Clint said, "but I'll probably just pay for my meals as I eat them."

"Yes, sir," Steve said, "as you wish."

Clint waved a hand and walked over to the entrance of the dining room. As he peered in, he saw that the place was very busy, but he spotted several empty tables.

When a man in a tuxedo approached him, Clint said, "I'd like that table," pointing to one against the wall.

"Are you a guest of the hotel, sir?"

"Yes, I am."

The white-haired man bowed at the waist and said, "Follow me, sir."

Clint followed him to the table he'd requested. The man allowed Clint to sit, then tried to put his napkin in his lap.

"That's okay," Clint said, grabbing the napkin, "I've got it."

"Yes, sir," the man said, with no offense taken. "I'll send your waiter right over."

"Thank you."

When the waiter came, Clint ordered a steak dinner and a pitcher of beer.

"Would you like to sign the check to your room, sir?" the man asked.

"No," Clint said, "I'll pay."

"As you wish, sir."

The waiter left, returned first with the pitcher of beer and a mug, and then with the dinner platter. Clint cut into the steak and found the first bite acceptable, possibly because he was particularly hungry.

He commenced eating with gusto.

Henry Frick's business was steel.

Ever since the building of the Eads Bridge in Saint Louis—the first bridge ever built from steel—steel had become one of the most valuable commodities in the country. Frick had partnered with Dale Carnegie, and the two rich men were becoming increasingly richer.

The bellboy found Frick in his office, but wasn't allowed to see him. He was stopped at the desk of the man's secretary.

"I'm supposed to deliver this personally," he told her.

"Giving it to me is delivering it personally," she assured him.

"I don't know . . ."

She extended her hand and said, "I do."

He stared at her for a few moments, then gave in and handed it over.

"Thank you," she said.

He remained standing there, obviously expecting a tip.

"I presume the man who sent the message will take care of you," she said.

"Uh, well, yeah."

"Then off you go."

He frowned, then turned and left.

The woman stood up, went to her boss's door, and knocked.

"Come!"

She opened the door and entered.

*   *   *

Henry Clay Frick was in his mid-thirties. While he sat at
the helm of his own company, H. C. Frick & Company, he
was also the chairman of the Carnegie Steel Company.

He sat back in his chair and watched his attractive secretary as she walked toward his desk.

"A bellboy just left this for you," she said, handing him
the note.

He did not immediately read it.

"Bellboy from where?"

"The Steel House."

"All right," he said. "Thank you."

He watched her hips sway as she walked to the door
and left. Then and only then did he unfold the note, secure
in the knowledge that his secretary had not read it.

THREE

Clint took a walk after he finished his palatable, if rather unremarkable, meal. Later he'd ask the clerk for the names of those restaurants he'd mentioned.

When he returned from his walk, he was surprised to see an expensive hansom cab with brass lamps parked in front of the hotel. He didn't think anyone would come looking for him so soon.

He entered the lobby as nonchalantly as he could, heard someone call out his name. He turned to see a man walking toward him, wearing a black suit.

"Yes?"

"Sir," the man said. "I have a cab waiting for you outside."

"And why would that be?"

"Mr. Frick has invited you to supper."

"But I had a late lunch."

"Pardon my saying so, sir," the man said, "but you wouldn't want to miss this meal."

"Is that right?"

"Yes, sir."

"Then maybe I should change my clothes?"

"No, sir," the man said, "you'll be fine the way you are."

Clint followed the man out to the cab, entered as the driver held the door open for him.

Clint felt the cab draw to a stop, felt the carriage shift as the driver stepped down. Then the door opened and the man appeared.

"This way, sir."

Clint stepped out and found that they'd stopped in front of a restaurant called the Four Leaf Clover Steak House.

"Are the steaks good here?" he asked.

The driver turned to look at him and said, "They're excellent."

"Good."

"This way, sir."

As he followed the driver, they marched right past a doorman and a maître d'. They walked past diners seated at white tablecloth-covered tables, with expensive china and silverware. The diners were nattily attired—the men in well-tailored suits, the women in brightly colored dresses and gowns.

The driver led him to a table where a bearded man in his mid-thirties sat. There was a bottle of champagne on the table, in a bucket of ice, but it hadn't yet been opened. The man was holding a glass with some amber liquid in it.

As they approached, the man had the good manners to stand.

"Mr. Adams, please meet Mr. Henry Clay Frick."

"Mr. Adams!" Frick said, extending his hand. "Delighted, sir, absolutely delighted."

"Mr. Frick."

"Thank you so much for accepting my invitation to dine with me."

"Well," Clint said, "I've been told the steaks here are excellent."

"They are, they are!" Frick said, his eyes positively glittering. "Please, have a seat."

Clint nodded, sat as the driver held the chair for him.

"That'll be all, Jason," Frick said to the driver. "You can wait outside."

"Yes, sir. Enjoy your meal, gentlemen."

The driver withdrew, and a waiter approached.

"May I?" Frick asked Clint.

"Please."

"Two T-bone dinners, Carson," Frick said, "with everything. Onion?" he asked Clint.

"Smothered in them."

"Onions, as well," Frick said.

"Yes, sir," the waiter said. "Shall I open the champagne, sir?"

"We'll take care of that ourselves," Frick told him.

"As you wish, sir."

Frick's suit was impeccably tailored, probably cost more than a good horse. His shirt had been boiled to a blinding white.

"I understand you've just arrived in Pittsburgh," Frick said.

"Only just," Clint said.

"I hope you'll forgive me for accosting you so soon upon your arrival, but when I received word that you were here—"

"From someone at the hotel?" Clint asked.

"Yes," Frick said. "I like to know when people of note come to town."

"I see."

"And the Gunsmith," Frick went on, "well, who could be of more note than you?"

"Lots of people," Clint said.

"You're modest," Frick said. "Your reputation—your legend—has spread across the entire country."

"Mr. Frick," Clint said, "I don't mind letting you buy me an excellent steak dinner, but please stop talking about my reputation."

"As you wish, sir," Frick said. "I actually have a special reason for inviting you to dine with me, but why don't we leave that for after dinner."

"That suits me," Clint said.

The waiter brought their meals, and true to his word, Frick remained silent while they ate.

FOUR

"Well?" Frick asked later. "What's the verdict?"

Clint sat back in his chair and said, "That was one of the best steaks I ever had. No, not just the steak, but the whole dinner."

"And would you like dessert?"

"Do they have peach pie?"

"They have every pie imaginable," Frick assured him.

They asked the waiter for a slice of peach pie and a slice of apple, with coffee.

"Well," Clint said after one taste, "this pie and the coffee both live up to the rest of the meal."

"Good," Frick said, "I'm glad to hear that. And there are even better restaurants in Pittsburgh than this one."

"I find that hard to believe," Clint said.

"I'll show you," Frick said, "that is, if you stay in town long enough. What brought you here in the first place?"

"I just thought I'd come east for a while," Clint said. "It's been many years since I've been in Pittsburgh."

"Well," Frick said, "many things have changed. In fact, that's one thing I wanted to talk to you about."

"Yes," Clint said, "you did mention you had something you wanted to say to me. Since you've given me one of the best meals of my life, I suppose I can give a listen."

"Wonderful," Frick said. He finished his last bite of pie and sat back. "Do you know who I am? I mean, have you ever heard of me?"

"Mr. Frick," Clint said, "I know about the work that you and Mr. Carnegie have been doing. With steel, I mean."

"That's good," Frick said. "Well, several years ago some colleagues and I—and by that I mean about fifty of us—started a club near here, near South Fork, above the dam."

"A club?"

"It's called the South Fork Fishing and Hunting Club. It's very exclusive."

"Meaning it's only for the rich."

"Anyone can join," Frick said. "Anyone who can afford the club dues, that is, and who is approved."

"Meaning the rich."

"Do you have some resentment toward the wealthy, Mr. Adams?" Frick asked.

Clint took a moment before answering.

"Keeping in mind that it's my money that is buying you the dinner you just ate," Frick said lightly.

"I have resentment," Clint said, "toward rich people who misuse their money."

"Meaning?"

"Meaning they try to . . . gain power over a town . . . a state . . . and country even."

"You mean like someone who uses his money to try and take control of . . . the government?"

"I don't know," Clint said. "That sounds like we'd be talking about all politicians."

"Do you have something against politicians?"

"I have the same problem," Clint said. "The misuse of their power."

"And do you think that running an exclusive fishing and hunting club is a . . . misuse of power and wealth?"

"Not necessarily."

"Perhaps, then," Frick said, "you should take a closer look."

"How so?"

"I would like to invite you to visit the club as my guest," Frick said.

"Why?" Clint asked. "I don't have the money to join, even if I like it."

"There are instances when a person is asked to join, and the club dues are waived. It is a . . . special membership."

"And I would have to qualify for this?"

"Yes—but I am not asking you to apply. I am only asking you to come as a guest. Just to . . . see what we have, and what we do . . . and who we are."

Clint waited a moment, then asked Frick, "How's the food up there?"

The driver, Jason, took Clint back to his hotel.

"Thank you," Clint said as the man opened the door of the carriage.

"You're welcome, sir."

"Tell me, Jason . . . can I call you Jason?"

"Of course, sir."

"Have you been to the South Fork Fishing and Hunting Club?"

"I have had that honor, sir."

"Are you a member?"

"Oh, no, sir," Jason said. "I simply drive Mr. Frick to and from."

"Have you eaten there?"

"I have been fed in the kitchen, with the staff."

"Do you think I should accept the invitation to visit?" he asked.

"I believe you should be honored, sir."

"I see," Clint said. "Thank you, Jason."

The man bowed, climbed aboard the carriage, and drove off.

FIVE

After Jason left Clint at his hotel, he drove right back to the steak house to pick up Henry Frick.

"Where to, sir?" he asked, once he had installed his boss in the back of the carriage. He was looking down at him through the hatch in the ceiling of the carriage.

"The club, Jason," Frick said. "I have things to discuss with the members."

"Yes, sir. It will be late when we get there."

"They'll wait," Frick said, "and I will be spending the night there."

"As you wish, sir."

He closed the hatch and drove off.

Clint entered his room and hung his gun belt on the bedpost. He'd eaten a passable steak dinner and an excellent steak dinner, and he was quite full. He had a small bottle of whiskey in his bag, for medicinal purposes only, and took a sip, using the cap as a shot glass. He replaced the cap and stowed the bottle away.

He was sitting on the bed, boots off, thinking over his

dinner conversation with Henry Frick, when there was a knock at his door. He snatched the gun from his holster on the bedpost and walked to the door. He couldn't possibly count the number of times he had answered a knock at his door this way, gun in hand.

"Who is it?" he asked.

"Did you order a whore?" a woman's voice asked.

He opened the door, saw the slatternly-looking girl in the hall, and asked, "What did you say?"

She was wearing a blue dress that was almost falling off her, revealing her shoulders and most of her creamy breasts. Her face may have been pretty beneath the heavy powder and rouge. There was a phony beauty mark high on her right cheek that drew his eye. She had a lot of tousled auburn hair.

"You asked for a whore to come to your room," she said. "I'm here."

"I didn't—"

"Don't leave me standing out here in the hall, Adams," she hissed, keeping her voice low. "Jeremy sent me."

"Oh," he said, surprised, "oh, okay . . ." He backed away to let her enter, then peered out into the hall before closing the door.

He turned to face her and she said, in a totally different voice, "Can you point that somewhere else?"

"Oh, sorry."

She walked over to the window and peered out.

"Were you followed?" he asked, holstering the gun.

"Dressed like this? I never know." Turning away from the window, she tugged at the dress, which barely hid her considerable assets.

"So what's happened so far?" she asked. "Have you met Frick?"

"I have," he said. "He bought me an excellent dinner tonight."

"Where?"

"The Four Leaf Clover."

"Ohhh," she said, scrunching up her face, "I've always wanted to eat there." Even beneath the face paint, she suddenly looked younger.

"Maybe," he said, "after."

"Yeah," she said, folding her arms across her breasts, "maybe. What else?"

"He invited me to the club."

Her face brightened.

"Ah, that's what Jeremy Pike said we wanted to happen."

"Glad to hear it."

Pike was an agent of the U.S. Secret Service, a man Clint had met through his friend Jim West, a legendary agent. He'd recently worked with Pike on a counterfeiting case, and hadn't expected to hear from the man again so soon, but a telegram had summoned him to Pittsburgh.

"Where is Jeremy?" Clint asked.

"Damned if I know," she said. "I got instructions to meet you here and talk."

"Well, then," he said, "tell me something useful."

"You got a drink?"

"Yeah."

He took the bottle of whiskey from his bag, poured some into the cap, and handed it to her.

"Sorry," he said, "no glass."

"This is fine," she told him, accepting it. She drank it down, wiped her mouth with the back of her hand, and handed the cap back.

"Another?"

"No, I'm good."

He capped the bottle and put it away.

"None for you?"

"I prefer beer."
"Then why carry the whiskey?"
"Medicinal purposes."
He closed the bag and set it aside.
"Have a seat," he invited, "and we'll talk."

SIX

She sat on the bed.

"What shall we talk about?"

"You tell me."

"Sit," she said. "There's room for both of us."

But instead of sitting on the bed, he pulled over a chair and sat across from her. She kept her arms folded, but instead of hiding her breasts, the gesture pushed them up. He pulled his eyes away and looked at her face.

"I have to admit, Adams, Pike really hasn't told me much."

"Aren't you working with him?"

"We work for the same people," she said. "I'm here because I was working on something else, which I eventually resolved. But before I could head back to Washington, I got a message telling me to remain in character, and make contact with you."

"Character?"

"Lizzie, the whore," she said. "This isn't who I really am."

"No, of course not."

"This dirt comes off," she said. "So does this dress."

"Um—"

"Okay," she said, "I didn't mean it that way. Anyway, I thought you were working with him on this—whatever this is."

"You don't know?" Clint said.

She shrugged. "I thought you did."

"But you know Frick's name."

"So do you."

Clint sat back in his chair.

"I've met with the man, but I don't know why," he said. "I've been invited to go to his private club in South Fork."

"Wow," she said. "I know about those clubs. Rich people only."

"Is this why I'm here?" he wondered aloud. "To accept that invitation?"

"Search me."

He realized he was once again looking at her breasts, and tore his eyes away.

"Do you know how to contact Jeremy?" he asked.

"I know how to leave him a message."

"Okay," Clint said. "Do it."

"And what do you want the message to say?"

"Have it say, 'What the hell am I supposed to do now?'" he told her.

When Henry Frick reached the South Fork Fishing and Hunting Club, he found his four closest colleagues waiting for him in one of the meeting rooms.

The four men turned as he entered. They were all holding glasses of brandy.

"You're late," Evan Lawrence said. In this early fifties, he was the youngest of the four members, and he sat on the club board. The others were all over sixty.

"Yes, well," Frick said, "we talked longer than I thought we would. For a man with his reputation as a pistoleer, he's remarkably intelligent."

"Is that so?" William Bledsoe said. "I thought Western gunmen were all mental deficients."

"Not so, apparently," Frick said.

"Well," Cole Foster asked, "did he agree to join?"

"No," Frick said. "In fact, he's still considering my invitation to come and see the place."

"The man's mad," Frederick Upton pronounced. "Do you know how many men of position would jump at the chance?"

"I know, yes," Frick said, pouring himself a brandy because there was no waiter available at this hour, "but he obviously does not."

"So is this going to work?" Foster asked. At seventy-one, he was the senior member of the group.

"I don't know," Frick said. "We'll have to wait and see."

"When will he give you his answer?" Lawrence asked.

"Tomorrow morning over breakfast, I hope," Frick said. "If he does, I'll bring him right up here."

"And if he doesn't?" Bledsoe asked.

"Then I'll keep working on him," Frick said.

"Well," Foster said testily, "I guess I could have stayed home and slept in my own bed."

"Sorry for that, Cole," Frick said.

"I'll say good night to you all," Foster said. He set his glass aside and walked slowly from the room.

"We're going to have to replace him, you know," Lawrence said.

"That's a discussion we can table for another time," Frick said.

"What about Carnegie?" Bledsoe asked. "Will he be coming here soon?"

"I'm still waiting to hear from Dale," Frick said.

"Rumor has it that you two have had a falling-out," Upton said.

"I think if Dale Carnegie and I had a falling-out," Frick said, "I would know about it."

It grew awkwardly silent before Lawrence said, "I suppose we all better turn in."

"I'll just finish this drink first," Frick said. "Good night."

The rest of them left the room while Frick sat and brooded over his drink.

SEVEN

Clint could feel the heat coming off Lizzie's body.

"I can send this message out tomorrow morning," she told him.

"Good," Clint said. "Frick expects an answer from me in the morning. I think he's going to buy me breakfast."

"At least you're getting some good meals out of the job."

"Not eating well?"

"Well," she said, tugging her dress down over her thighs—and almost exposing her breasts—"I'm not exactly losing weight."

"Obviously not."

She glared at him.

"Is that a smart remark at my expense?"

"Not at all," he said. "If this was your regular line of work, I'm sure you'd be in high demand."

That comment seemed to mollify her a bit, but she said, "The competition around here is rather meager."

"Listen," he said, "I've got an indoor water closet here. Would you like to use it?"

"At the moment a flush toilet doesn't interest me much."

"I was thinking more of the bathtub."

That perked her up.

"A bathtub?"

"It's all yours if you want."

She seemed to be considering the proposal.

"No strings attached, of course," he added.

"You know," she said, rubbing her hands over her bare upper arms, "I think I'll take you up on that."

"Why don't I draw it for you?" he suggested. "Hot?"

"Of course."

While she was soaking in the tub, Clint knocked on the door.

"Yes?"

"I have some towels and a robe," he said.

"Bring them in."

"Are you sure?" he asked. "I could just set them down out here—"

"Don't be an old poop," she said. "Bring them in."

He opened the door and entered, carrying the robe and towels. The room was filled with steam, as she had asked for the water to be extra hot. The air was also filled with the smell of the scented soap the hotel supplied.

Lizzie was immersed in the water up to her neck, except for one leg, which she had extended, the heel resting on the edge of the tub. He wondered if that was for his benefit. If it was, he appreciated it. It was a lovely, well-muscled leg.

There was a chair in the corner. He walked to it and set down the robe and towels.

"Do you have enough soap?" he asked.

"I do, thank you."

"Is the water still hot?"

"Quite hot. Why do you keep averting your eyes?"

"I'm trying to be a gentleman," he said. "And let me tell you, it's not easy."

"Then stop it," she said. "I don't want you to hurt yourself."

He turned his head and looked at her. She had raised herself up a bit, and dropped her leg into the water. In that position, a good portion of her breasts showed, with just a hint of nipples. That was a lot of supple, shiny-wet flesh.

"Thank you for the towels and robe," she said. "I should be out soon."

"Take your time," he told her. "Would you like some food?"

"I have nothing to wear to the dining room," she told him.

"I'll go downstairs and bring something up for you."

"You'd do that?"

"Sure," he said. "A steak?"

"You know," she said, shifting so that most of her brown nipples now showed, "a bowl of beef stew would really hit the spot right now."

"And what would the lady like to drink with it?"

"Do they have any brandy?"

"I'm sure they do."

"That would be great."

"All right," he said. "I'll go down now and be back as soon as I can. You just continue to soak."

"Thank you, Adams."

"Clint," he said. "Just call me Clint."

"All right," she said. "Clint."

"See you soon."

He left the water closet and the room, and went downstairs to the lobby.

* * *

The dining room was about to close, but the waiter was happy to get Clint a bowl of stew and a bottle of brandy to take to his room.

"How about some biscuits?" the waiter offered.

"That'd be great. Thanks."

"We like to see to all our guests' needs if we can, sir."

"Well," Clint said, "so far you're doing a great job of it."

EIGHT

When he got back to the room with the food, Lizzie was still in the water closet. He pulled a table and chair to the center of the room, and set the food on it, then went to the water closet door and knocked.

"I'm back."

"I'll be right out."

As an afterthought, he set a second chair at the table. He hadn't gotten any food for himself, but he could have a glass of brandy with her.

The water closet door opened and she came out, wearing the robe and drying her hair with one of the towels. The robe revealed a good portion of her legs, and some cleavage.

"That smells wonderful," she said. "I don't know how to thank you."

"Madam," he said, pulling out her chair, "your table."

She set the towel aside and said, "Thank you, sir."

With the face paint washed off, she was pretty, and looked much younger.

"Are you eating?" she asked when she was seated.

"I've eaten enough today," he said, "but I'll have a glass of brandy with you. If you don't mind talking while you eat."

"I don't mind at all. Oh, biscuits!" She grabbed the basket.

Clint poured the brandy and watched the woman eat. She had a healthy appetite, and attacked the food with gusto, cleaning the bowl with the biscuits.

She sat back and noticed him watching her.

"Hey," she said, "I'm a big girl, and I eat like one."

"I wasn't being critical," he said. "I like a girl with an appetite."

She reached for her brandy glass.

"You know," he said, "you look a lot better without all that face paint."

She touched her face and said, "I know. It makes me look older and harder, though. That's how I need to look."

"How long are you supposed to be working this disguise?" he asked.

"I was supposed to be back in Washington a week ago," she said. "Pike's message caught me before I could leave."

"Well, then," Clint said, "I guess neither one of us knows how long we'll be here."

"I don't like being in the dark," she said, hunching her shoulders.

The soft woman seated in front of him was quite different from the brassy whore who had appeared at his door. This was also the first time he felt she might be frightened.

"Where are you staying?" he asked.

"In a cheap hotel down by the water," she said. "My budget for this assignment didn't allow me much more than that."

"Well," Clint said, "since I'm feeling like we're partners in this, you can spend the night here, if you want."

She looked over at the one bed in the room.

"You can have the bed," he assured her. "In fact, I can go and get myself another room."

"No," she said, "that would look too suspicious, if anyone's watching. I mean, if I stayed, it would have to look like I'm doing my job, you know?"

"Well, all right," he said. "I can sleep in a chair, or on the floor. You can have the bed. Nobody outside this room will know."

She hunched her shoulders again and said, "It's very tempting."

"I get the feeling you've worked hard and deserve a night in a big, comfortable bed."

"You have no idea," she said, rolling her eyes. "The mattress I've been sleeping on is paper thin."

"Then it's settled," he said. "You'll take the bed."

"Thank you," she said. "I'll make sure I get up early enough to send that message to Pike for you."

"Thanks," Clint said. "I'd like to get a little guidance about what I'm supposed to do here."

She stood up and said, "It's amazing that you'd even come here without knowing what's expected of you."

"I have a habit," he said, moving the table and chair away from the center of the room, "of responding to telegrams and messages from friends—or from my country. Some might say it's a bad habit."

"Well," she said, "I know I'm getting paid for my part. I can't imagine doing this for free."

"I'm sure the money isn't all of it for you," he said. "I know what civil servants get paid."

She walked to the bed, turned it down, and sat on it.

"Wow," she said, "this is going to be like sleeping on a cloud." She looked over at him and said, "I feel bad putting you out of your bed."

"Don't feel bad," he said. "I'm used to sleeping on hard surfaces."

"Well," she said, "it'll only be for one night."

Suddenly, as he looked at her, he noticed her eyelids getting very heavy.

"You might as well turn in now, before you fall over," he said.

She slid between the sheets and said, "Don't worry about the light. It won't . . ." Her voice trailed off and then Clint heard a faint snore.

NINE

Clint was uncomfortable on the chair, and on the floor, but he tried not to move around very much. Lizzie was sleeping soundly and he didn't want to wake her. That's why he was surprised when he heard her voice.

"You can't be comfortable over there," she said from beneath the covers.

"I'm fine," he assured her.

"No, you're not," she said. "Come on. There's plenty of room in this bed."

"I don't think—"

"Don't worry," she said, "I won't attack your lily-white body."

He stood up from the chair and stretched.

"Yeah, okay," he said, approaching the bed.

She tossed back the sheets on the other side of the bed and said, "Hey, you're not getting into bed with your clothes on. You don't have to be naked, but for Chrissake, get comfortable."

"Yeah, okay."

It was dark in the room, but they both had pretty good

night vision. He could see her lying in the bed, but not if her eyes were open or closed.

He removed his shirt, and then his trousers. Clad only in his underwear, he got into the bed and covered himself with the sheets. Before he was done, she was already snoring again.

In a saloon near the docks, two men sat at a back table, as far away from the door and windows as they could get. Only one of them wore a gun, but the second had an armed bodyguard standing at the bar.

"This is not exactly the kind of place I meant when I said we had to meet secretly."

"We ain't gonna be seen here."

"Yes, all right," the well-dressed man said. He looked around, feeling distinctly uncomfortable. "What did you find out?"

"I took a look at the dam," the other man said. "It's springing leaks. Lots of them."

"Can it be fixed?"

"Well, yeah—"

"Cheaply?"

"Now that might be a problem."

"Look," the well-dressed man said, "you're supposed to be an engineer."

"I am an engineer," the man said. "I built most of the Union's dams and bridges during the war."

"Yes, well, that was a long time ago," the other man said. "These days you wear a gun and you use it. But that's not what I hired you for."

"What did you hire me for exactly?"

The well-dressed man leaned forward and said, "I want the holes in that dam plugged."

"Cheaply."

"Correct," the man said. "I'm not going to drain the club's coffers—or my own—to fix that dam. Get it?"

"I get it," the engineer said. "I'll do the best I can."

The other man stood up and said, "Do better than that. Do what I'm paying you to do."

He walked to the bar to fetch his bodyguard, and they left the saloon together.

After the well-dressed man left, two other men joined the engineer at his table, carrying beers of their own and a fresh one for him.

"How'd that go?" Kevin Dale asked, taking the vacated seat.

"Not well."

"Ain't we gettin' paid?" Frank Conlin asked.

"Oh, we'll get paid," the engineer said. "I just have to find a way to plug that dam."

"With the money they have to throw around, that should be pretty easy," Dale said.

"Yeah," the engineer said, "but they don't exactly want to throw that money around."

"Then how do they expect you to fix it?" Kevin Dale inquired.

"Maybe like the little boy."

"What little boy?" Conlin asked.

"The one who put his finger in the dike."

Conlin looked confused.

"I'll explain it to you later," Dale said to him. He looked at his boss. "So what do we do now?"

"We take another look at that dam," the engineer said. "See what we can see."

"And then what?" Conlin asked.

"And then we see just how cheaply it can be fixed."

"Boy," Conlin said, "why are such rich men so cheap?"

"I guess," the engineer said, "that's how rich men stay rich."

TEN

Clint woke to a hand on his chest. For a moment he thought it might be an accident, that Lizzie had rolled over and draped her arm over him. But when the hand started to rub his chest, and he felt those big breasts against his back, the nipples poking at him, he knew it wasn't.

"You said you wouldn't attack my lily-white body," he reminded her.

She slid her hand down his chest, over his belly, to his crotch, where she gripped him tightly.

"Oh my," she said, stroking him. "It looks like I lied."

"Lizzie—"

"Don't worry, Clint," she said, pressing her lips to his back, "the whore getup is just a disguise. I haven't been with a man for a long time . . . and we're kind of close here."

"But you had a bath and I didn't."

She pressed her nose to him and said, "You smell like a man. That's fine with me."

"Well, if that's the case . . ." he said, and rolled over . . .

*   *   *

The engineer's name was Dash Charles.

He had, indeed, been an engineer during the war, even though he'd been only nineteen when called. Actually, he built bridges and dams and walls while in the Army, and got the education afterward. But by the time he was educated as an engineer, those kinds of jobs had mostly dried up. That was when he took to the gun.

These days, he was trying to combine the two jobs, gunman and engineer. He'd stumbled into Pittsburgh, and this job, where the man who hired him was interested in both of his professions.

After he left the saloon and his two colleagues, Dale and Conlin, he went back to his hotel, which was nowhere near the docks. He may not have minded drinking there, but he didn't want to stay in any of the hotels located there. They were bug-infested flophouses.

He was being paid well for this job, so he was able to stay in a better hotel, like the Colonial, which had three floors, a big lobby, and clean rooms. He'd asked for and received a room on the top floor, where he didn't have to worry about anyone climbing in a window.

He let himself in with his key, and the girl on the bed came off and into his arms.

"I missed you!" she exclaimed. She grabbed his crotch. "I missed this! Come on."

"Take it easy," he said. "I'm an old man, remember."

The girl's name was Bonnie, and she was twenty-three.

"Not so old," she said, stroking him through his trousers. "Look, he's already awake."

He removed his gun belt and she hurriedly undid his trousers and dragged them to his ankles. She dropped to her knees before him and gobbled his cock eagerly.

"Jesus . . ." he breathed, holding the back of her head

while she sucked him, wondering if what she really missed was his wallet.

Clint slid his arms around Lizzie and kissed her. She moaned, entwined her legs with his. She smelled sweet of the soap she'd bathed with. He kissed her deeply, ran his hands over her body, down her back to her buttocks, which he clutched as he pulled her to him.

"Damn, damn," she breathed into his mouth. "Don't go slow. Come on."

She broke from his arms and rolled onto her back, opening her legs.

He rolled on top of her, and then was inside her. She was so wet there was no resistance at all.

"Come on," she said, "it's been so long, just plough me!"

Music to any man's ears . . .

Charles slapped Bonnie on the ass as he fucked her from behind. He liked making love to a girl face-to-face, but she told him that was old-fashioned. She showed him her bare ass and said, "This is how they do it now!"

But before he finished, he flipped her over onto her back and rammed himself into her. Old-fashioned or not, she was going to get fucked on her back and like it . . .

Clint looked down at the top of Lizzie's head as she sucked him. Once she'd screamed and orgasmed the first time, she'd pushed him onto his back and taken his cock into her mouth. She may not have been with a man for a long while, but she was still good at it. She suckled him, and stroked him, and squeezed his balls, and kept him from finishing until she was good and ready, and when he exploded into her mouth, he roared loudly enough to wake the entire hotel . . .

ELEVEN

In the morning, true to her word, Lizzie woke up early and donned her dress. It looked rather incongruous on her, without the face paint.

Clint started to get up, but she put her hand on his chest and pushed him down.

"Don't," she said. "You need to sleep. I'll get that message sent off."

"Will I see you again?"

She shrugged.

"I don't know," she said. "I guess that depends on how things go. I might have to go back to Washington."

"Right, right."

She leaned over again and kissed him.

"Thanks for everything," she said. "The bath, the meal, the bed . . . everything . . . you didn't have to . . ."

"That's okay," he said. "Be careful out there."

"I will," she said. "I'm always careful."

He watched her go out the door, then lay back in the bed, which smelled of her. Meeting her had been unexpected but, in the end, pleasurable. But she had been able to tell him little about why he was there. For that, he needed to talk to Jeremy Pike, if and when he showed up.

He went back to sleep.

A couple of hours later he got himself up and dressed and down to the lobby. Henry Frick was nowhere to be seen. He went to the front desk to address the same clerk who had checked him in.

"Any messages for me?"

"Uh, no, sir," the clerk said. "Let me check again." He looked in the message box for Clint's room. "No, sir, I'm afraid not."

Clint went into the dining room for breakfast. The eggs were kind of runny but the bacon was nice and crispy and the coffee was hot and strong.

He was having a second pot of coffee, and another full rasher of bacon, when Frick walked in. He still hadn't heard a word from Lizzie or Pike.

Frick saw him and crossed the room to his table.

"I was going to take you somewhere a little better for breakfast."

"As it turns out, this was good enough," Clint said. "Good coffee and bacon."

Frick looked at the remnants of the eggs in Clint's plate.

"Bad eggs?" he asked.

"Bad eggs."

Frick sat down.

"Coffee?" Clint asked.

"Yes, thanks."

Clint poured Frick a cup, then topped his own off.

"Have you decided?" Frick asked.

"Decided what?"

"What we talked about last night," Frick said. "Coming to see the club."

"Oh, well . . ." Clint saw the clerk appear in the doorway, and then start toward them. He was carrying something in his hand.

"Sir?" he said. "A message just came to you. It was given to me by a wo—"

"Thank you," Clint said, cutting him off. "I'll take it."

"Yes, sir, of course."

The clerk handed over the message, turned, and left.

"Important?" Frick asked.

"Who knows? Excuse me." Clint opened the message, read it, then tucked it away in his pocket.

"So?" Frick asked. "Important?"

"A woman."

"Ah," Frick said. "A lady?"

"A girl," Clint said.

"Ah," Frick said. "You could bring her with you, you know. It would impress her."

"No, that's all right," Clint said. "I think I did that on my own."

"Oh," he said. "Well done, then."

Clint put a crispy piece of bacon into his mouth, then pushed the plate toward Frick.

"Help yourself."

"Thanks," Frick said, taking one.

"Do you want to have breakfast while we talk?" Clint asked.

"Yes, I do," Frick said, chewing. "I haven't had a thing yet."

Clint waved the waiter over.

"Stay away from the eggs," Clint reminded him.

"Flapjacks," Frick told the waiter.

"Yes, sir, coming up."

They didn't talk until Frick's breakfast had come, and Clint poured him some more coffee.

"I've spoken with my colleagues at the club," Frick said. "They're excited about the possibility of your coming up. You know, these aren't half bad."

"I'm glad," Clint said. "Look, why don't we go up to see your club this afternoon?"

"Today? Excellent!" Frick said. "I have my carriage. We could go right from here—"

"I think this afternoon would be better," Clint said. "I've got something else to do this morning."

"Ah," Frick said, "the girl?"

Clint nodded and said, "The girl."

"Very well," Frick said. "Why don't I come by and pick you up around one?"

"That'll be good," Clint said.

"It's settled, then," Frick said, and went back to his flapjacks.

They walked out of the hotel together, stopped just outside the door.

"I'll pick you up right here, then," Frick said.

Clint looked over at Frick's carriage, where the driver, Jason, was waiting.

"Yes," Clint said, "right here."

"Excellent!"

Frick shook Clint's hand, walked to his carriage, and got in. Jason looked back at Clint, nodded, and drove away.

TWELVE

Clint got himself a cab and gave the driver the name written in the message, which said, "Agree to go to the club, and meet me at Solomon's Saloon . . ."

"Solomon's?" the driver asked, obviously recognizing the name.

"That's right."

"On Wylie Avenue?"

"If that's where it is."

"Are you sure?"

"I'm sure."

The young driver shrugged and said, "Suit yourself."

When the carriage pulled to a stop in front of the saloon, it looked fine to Clint. He didn't know why the driver was so concerned with him going there.

He paid the man and said, "Thanks."

"Good luck," the driver said, and drove off.

Clint went in the door and stopped just inside. The place was small, clean, all dark wood and gleaming gold. In a corner he saw Jeremy Pike sitting alone. He studied the rest of the tables, but nobody was paying any attention to him. He walked to Pike's table and sat down. A bartender appeared suddenly and placed a beer at his elbow.

"Thanks, Kenny," Pike said.

"I didn't expect to hear from you so soon after the counterfeiting case," Clint said. "Did you ever find Ninger?"

Emanuel Ninger was a notorious German counterfeiter working out of Saint Louis. Pike and Clint had managed to shut down his operation, but the man himself had eluded them.

"Actually, we're still looking for him," Pike said, "but I got involved with something else."

"The South Fork Fishing and Hunting Club?"

"Yeah."

"What's going on up there?"

"We don't know," Pike said. "We've been trying to get up there, but have had no luck."

"Why me, then?"

"Have you been invited?"

"I have."

"That answers your question, then," Pike said. "We thought you might be."

"We?"

"Well, me," Pike said. "I suggested it. We had just seen each other in Saint Louis, so it occurred to me that you were the kind of person a hunting club would invite to join. Are you going up there?"

"Yeah, this afternoon."

"Good."

"What am I looking for, Jeremy?"

"Not sure," Pike said. "Anything . . . suspicious."

"What could be suspicious?"

"Don't know," Pike said, "but there are a lot of rich men up there, lots of political clout among them—"

"Is this about politics?"

"If it is," Pike said, "I won't ask you to go any further. I know how you feel about politics."

"All right," Clint said. "Frick is going to pick me up at one."

"Good."

They each drank down some of their beer, and then caught up a bit on what they'd been doing since Saint Louis.

"Oh," Clint said, then, "I met Lizzie."

"Lizzie?"

"The girl you sent to my hotel, dressed as a whore."

Pike shook his head.

"I didn't send anybody to see you," Pike said. "Not a whore or anybody. The message I sent this morning was the first contact."

"But the clerk said a woman delivered it," Clint said.

"Yeah," Pike said, "I just paid a girl from here to drop it off."

"What's her name?"

"Mary, I think."

"What's she look like?"

"Small, mousy, brown hair. She works here as a waitress. That the girl you're talking about?"

"No," Clint said. "This was a big girl, about five foot eight, very appealing."

"A whore?"

"She said she was disguised as a whore, and that you sent her to me."

"Me?" Pike asked. "She mentioned me by name?"

"She did."

"Oh," Pike said, "I don't like this at all."

"How long have you been in Pittsburgh?" Clint asked.

"A few days."

"And you never ran across a girl like that?"

"No. What did she say her name was?"

"Lizzie," Clint said. "Just Lizzie."

"No last name?"

"We never got that far."

"Are you supposed to see her again?"

"I don't know," Clint said. "She said that depended on you, and on whether or not she got called back to Washington."

"Well," Pike said, "if you do hear from her again, you can ask her who the hell she is and how she knows my name."

"I'll do that," Clint said. "Does this change what you want me to do?"

"No," Pike said. "Go ahead and go to the club with Frick, see what you can see. Meet me here again tomorrow, same time. Is that okay?"

"Sure."

"Clint," Pike said, "thanks for coming when I sent that telegram."

"You said you need help," Clint said. "I assumed West and Gordon were unavailable again."

"The government is keeping them real busy," Pike said. "That's why I'm getting more assignments like this."

"They should assign you a partner."

"Yes, they should."

Clint sat back, looked around the room. There was still nobody paying much attention to them.

"So what's wrong with this place?" he asked.

"What?" Pike asked. "Nothing. What makes you think something's wrong with it?"

"My cab driver was surprised I wanted to come here. When he dropped me off, he wished me luck."

"That's odd," Pike said. "Maybe he just didn't think it was your kind of place."

Clint studied Pike's impeccably tailored suit, and his own worn clothing.

"I think I better go and buy some new clothes," he said.

THIRTEEN

Clint was standing in front of his hotel when Henry Frick's carriage pulled up. The driver, Jason, stepped down from the seat and approached.

"Mr. Adams," he said. "Are you ready?"

"Is Mr. Frick in the carriage?"

"Unfortunately, Mr. Frick is not here. He had to go ahead to the club. But I'm authorized to drive you up there."

"Then I guess you'd better drive. Is what I'm wearing all right?"

"You bought new clothing," Jason said. "Yes, it's fine—but . . ."

"But what?"

"The gun," Jason said. "You won't need that."

"The gun goes where I go," Clint said. "Always."

"I see," Jason said. "Very well, then. Shall we go?"

"By all means," Clint said, "let's go."

He followed Jason to the carriage, where the man held the door open for him. When Clint was inside, he felt Jason climb aboard, and then they were moving.

*   *   *

The ride to the South Fork Fishing and Hunting Club took them past Lake Conemaugh and the South Fork dam.

"That was a lot of water back there," Clint said as he stepped down from the carriage.

"Yes, sir," Jason said. "The club owns the dam and is responsible for maintaining it."

"Is that right?"

"Yes, sir," Jason said. "This way."

Clint followed Jason up a long, winding walk to the front entrance of the club. The building was sprawling, probably covering several acres, not to mention the grounds around it.

"This place is huge," Clint said.

"Yes, sir," Jason said, "very impressive."

Unless you compared it to some of the huge, sprawling ranches Clint had seen over the years. He much preferred those open spaces to this.

They entered the building and Clint found himself in a high-ceilinged entry hall.

"Perhaps you should wait here, sir," Jason said, "while I find . . . somebody."

"Sure," Clint said, "I'll wait here and you go find somebody."

Jason nodded and went off into the building, leaving Clint alone.

Clint remained alone for fifteen minutes, with not much to look at but the high-beamed ceilings and the view out the front windows. Also mounted on the walls were some stuffed heads, both deer and bear. He assumed these were some of the members' trophies.

Abruptly he heard returning footsteps, then saw Henry Frick followed by Jason.

"Clint," he said, "I'm so sorry I couldn't meet you at the hotel. Something came up." He extended his hand and shook Clint's firmly.

"That's all right," Clint said. "I managed to make it, thanks to Jason."

"Ah yes, Jason," Frick said. He turned and looked up at the big man. "That'll be all, Jason. You can see to the carriage and horse now."

"Yes, sir."

The big man went out the front door without a further word, or even a look.

"Come this way," Frick said to Clint. "Some of the members would like to meet you."

"Lead the way," Clint said.

FOURTEEN

Frick led Clint to a large, wood-paneled room, furnished with leather armchairs, several of which were occupied at that moment.

"Gentlemen," Frick said, "allow me to introduce you to our guest, Mr. Clint Adams."

The four men all stood. Three of them had congenial looks on their faces while the fourth—the oldest—seemed to be feeling rather crotchety.

"Welcome," one man said. "My name is Evan Lawrence." They shook hands.

Clint then shook hands with the other men—William Bledsoe, Cole Foster, and Frederick Upton. Foster was the older, sour-looking man.

"Please," Frick said, "have a seat. Can we offer you a brandy?"

"Sure, why not?"

Frick supplied Clint with a glass, and then they all seated themselves.

"We're quite excited to have you as a guest, Mr. Adams," Lawrence said.

"It's nice of you all to allow me up here," Clint said. "I understand it's very . . . private."

"It is that," Bledsoe said, "but a man of your caliber . . ." He left the rest unsaid.

"Well, I appreciate it," Clint said, even though he never would have been a member of such an elitist club.

"How long do you plan to be in the area, Mr. Adams?" Bledsoe asked.

"I'm not sure," Clint said. "I guess that depends on how long I can entertain myself."

"Well," Upton said, "perhaps we can be the ones to do the entertaining."

Clint raised his glass in response.

After they chatted and Clint had finished his drink, Henry Frick said, "Perhaps I should give Clint the tour." They both stood up.

"You'll stay for lunch with some of the other members," Upton said.

"Of course," Clint said. "Thank you for the offer."

He followed Frick from the room.

"I'll show you the building," he said. "We have a lot of room. And then I'll show you some of the hunting grounds we have."

"On the way here we passed the lake and the dam," Clint said. "Jason told me the club owns the dam."

"That is true."

"I'd like to see it."

"The dam?" Frick asked, surprised. "Why would you want to see that?"

"I'm interested," Clint said.

"You're interests are varied, then."

"They are," Clint said. "Is there some reason I shouldn't see the dam and lake?"

"No, no," Frick said, "let me walk you through the buildings, and then we can have Jason drive us around the grounds. We'll finish at the dam, and then come back here for lunch."

"Sounds like a plan to me," Clint said.

After Frick and Clint left the room, Cole Foster said, "I don't like him."

Lawrence looked at the old man and said, "You don't like anybody these days, Cole."

"Well, then," Foster said sourly, "put him at the top of the list."

FIFTEEN

Henry Frick walked Clint through the entire building, showing him meeting rooms, game rooms, exercise rooms, dining rooms, and bedrooms. Of special interest to Clint in one of the game rooms was a green felt-topped poker table.

"Is there a lot of poker played by the members?" he asked.

"Some of our members are very keen on poker," Frick said. "I don't see the appeal myself, but I understand you have a reputation as a player."

"I enjoy the game," Clint admitted.

"Well," Frick said, "perhaps we can arrange a contest for you with some of the members."

"That would be interesting," Clint said.

Frick took Clint around the outside of the building, showing him several balconies and patios, and then the expanse of land that stretched out behind the building.

"We have all kinds of game," he said. "Are you a hunter?"

"Not for sport," Clint said. "I usually eat what I hunt."

"Living in the West as you do, I can understand that," Frick said. "I'm sure you saw the mounted heads in our lobby. And throughout the building."

"Yes," Clint said. "Mounted heads don't tend to impress me."

"I can understand that, too," Frick said. "Gambling and hunting hold no fascination for me. I am only interested in one thing."

"And what's that?"

"Making money."

Frick found Jason and had him hitch the horse up to the carriage once again. The big man drove them out to see the lake, and then took them to a good vantage point from where they could see the dam.

"Very impressive," Clint said. "How do you maintain it?"

"We have engineers on the payroll who take care of it," Frick said.

"I guess Johnstown would be in a lot of trouble if that dam ever broke."

"Which is why we keep the engineers on retainer," Frick said. "It's our responsibility to make sure that everyone who might be in the path of that water is safe."

They got back into the carriage and rode back to the main complex for lunch.

They had lunch in a large dining room with a long table that accommodated about twenty club members, plus the Gunsmith. Lunch consisted of pheasant and vegetables, and chocolate mousse for dessert.

"The club is quite proud of our chef," Henry Frick told Clint.

Clint didn't know where they managed to find pheasant. They were more likely to find wild turkeys on their hunting preserve.

"It's very good," Clint said, even though he much preferred beef.

Frick was seated on Clint's left. On his right and across from him were club members he had not met before. They questioned him about his reputation, questions which he skillfully managed to avoid answering. He turned it around so that he was able to get some information from them. They were all rich, and had rich men's egos. By the time lunch was finished, Clint knew quite a bit about them—bankers, industrialists, lawyers, businessmen.

Afterward they took Clint to another lounge for cigars and brandy with Frick and the men Clint soon realized were Frick's inner circle.

"So," Lawrence asked, "what did you think of our club today?"

"I have to say," Clint said, "I was impressed."

"With what specifically?" Old Man Foster asked.

"Well . . . the dam, for one thing."

"The dam?" Bledsoe asked. "Why on earth would you be impressed with the dam?"

"It's quite an achievement," Clint said, "and it keeps a lot of people safe. And . . . it's the responsibility of the club to keep it strong."

"There are many other aspects of our club that we're proud of, much more than the dam," Upton said. "The hunting, for one thing."

"I'm not much of a hunter," Clint said. "As I told Mr. Frick, I usually eat what I hunt."

"Have you ever killed a bear?" Foster asked.

"I have."

"You didn't eat it, I'm sure."

"No," Clint said, "I killed that bear in order to stay alive."

"So you've never mounted any of your prey?" Frederick Upton asked.

"It's quite invigorating to see that head up on a wall, I must say," William Bledsoe added.

"Well," Clint said, "I've hunted quite a few men and sent them to jail."

Cole Foster frowned, looking even more sour than he usually did.

"In all my years, I've never hunted a man."

The rest of the members all seemed to be considering that comment.

"When I've hunted men," Clint said, "they've deserved to be hunted. They were killers who had to be punished."

"I'm sure they were," Frick said. "Are you ready to go back to Pittsburgh?"

"I think I'm ready," Clint said, putting his glass down. "It was a pleasure to meet you gents." He went around the room and shook hands with each of the men.

"This way, Clint," Frick said. "Jason is waiting out front with the carriage."

"Perhaps we can get you up here and show you how we hunt," Cole Foster said.

"We'll see," Clint said, although he doubted it very much. He had no desire to go hunting with any of these vain, wealthy men.

SIXTEEN

As was the case when he'd been picked up that afternoon, Frick did not accompany Clint on the return trip.

"I'm afraid we have a board meeting tonight, at which some very important matters will be discussed," Frick explained. "I can't afford to miss it."

"Of course."

"Jason will take you to your hotel. I will be back in town tomorrow, and perhaps we can have a drink together then. And discuss some . . . well, some matters that are still being decided."

"All right, Mr. Frick."

"Please," Frick said, extending his hand, "from this point on, just call me Henry."

"All right, Henry."

The two men shook hands and then Frick watched as Jason held the door of the carriage open for Clint. As the carriage pulled away, Clint did not look out the window, even though he felt sure Frick was still standing there, seeing him off.

He was happy not to be in the company of those men anymore.

Jason dropped Clint off in front of the hotel and was about to leave when Clint said, "Hey, Jason."

"Sir?"

"How about a drink?"

"Sir?"

"Have you got anything to do now?"

"No, sir," Jason said. "I was informed that I could go home after I left you off, and bring the carriage back to the club tomorrow."

"Okay, then," Clint said, "let me buy you a drink."

"Well . . . all right, sir."

"Come on," Clint said, "my hotel has a saloon."

"The carriage—"

"I'll talk to the doorman. He'll watch your carriage for you."

"All right, sir."

They walked to the door together, where Clint had a talk with the doorman and handed him some money.

"Don't worry, sir," the doorman assured him. "It'll be safe."

"Thanks."

Clint led Jason into the hotel lobby and through to the saloon.

"What'll you have?" Clint asked.

"A beer, sir."

"I'll get you a beer," Clint said, "but stop calling me 'sir.'"

"Yes, sir."

"Grab a table over there in the corner."

Clint went to the bar, got two mugs of beer from the bartender, and joined Jason at the table.

"Thank you, si—uh, thank you."

"So tell me," Clint said, "where is it that you do live? Not up at the club?"

"No," Jason said, "some of the members sleep up there sometimes, but no one really lives there."

"So you live in town?"

"Yes . . . I have a small house here in town that suits me just fine."

"And your job? Driving Frick? Is that all you do for a living?"

"I drive for Mr. Frick and some of the other club members," Jason said. "I am actually employed by the South Fork Fishing and Hunting Club."

"I see."

Clint sipped his beer and studied the man across from him. Jason looked to be in his thirties, stood well over six two or three. He spoke and dressed like an educated man.

"Maybe you can answer a question for me, Jason," Clint said.

"If I can."

"Why are the members so touchy when it comes to talking about the dam?"

"Are they?" Jason sipped at his beer while they talked, the volume of their voices getting lower and lower.

"I think they are," Clint said. "They want to talk about hunting and business, but when I brought up the dam, they were reluctant to say anything."

"It might be a sore subject for them," Jason said.

"Why would that be?"

"I'm not sure," Jason said. The man had drunk half his beer and seemed to be loosening up a bit.

"Come on," Clint said, "you must have some idea. Why don't you finish that beer and I'll get you another one."

Jason drank the beer down and said, "Sure, why not?"

Clint picked up the two empty mugs, walked to the bar, and came back with full ones.

"There you go," he said, putting them on the table and pushing one toward the driver.

The two men sat and drank . . .

SEVENTEEN

"The dam needs a lot of work," Jason said.

This was sometime later, after a few beers had crossed the table.

"Work?"

"It's been showing signs of wear."

"Don't they have engineers working on that?" Clint asked. "I mean, Mr. Frick told me they had several engineers on the payroll."

"They do," Jason said, "and I may be talking out of turn. After all, I am not an engineer. But I've seen that dam up close. It has some problems."

"You're saying there are structural problems that need to be addressed?"

"Yes," Jason said, "there are."

"Well," Clint said, "I'm sure the club is having their engineers address those problems, right?"

"Definitely," Jason said. He finished the beer in front of him and pushed the empty mug away.

"Another?" Clint asked.

"No, thank you," Jason said. "That's enough for me. I

must go home and turn in. I have to be at the club early tomorrow."

They walked to the lobby together and separated there, Jason thanking Clint one more time for the drinks.

The next afternoon Clint once again met with Jeremy Pike at Solomon's Saloon. Once again as he entered, none of the patrons seemed to pay any attention to him as he crossed to Pike's table.

"So," Pike asked after Clint had a drink in front of him, "how did your visit to the club go?"

"They tried very hard to impress me," Clint said.

"And did they succeed?"

"No," Clint said. "There are too many egos in that club. And they're too concerned with making money and putting trophies on the wall."

"Well," Pike said, "they're wealthy men, after all."

"That's true."

"Did you find out anything else?" Pike asked. "Notice anything?"

"I heard something, but I don't know if it would be of any interest to you, or the government."

"And what's that?"

"The dam," Clint said.

"What about it?"

"Apparently it needs some repairs."

"Isn't that what the club is supposed to do?" Pike asked. "Don't they have engineers for that?"

"They do," Clint said. "Frick told me that himself."

"So who told you it needed work?"

"Jason, the driver."

"The driver?" Pike said. "You mean . . . what? He drives the members where they want to go?"

"Exactly."

"So what does he know about dams?"

"Just what he sees," Clint said, "and he sees some structural problems."

Pike frowned.

"I don't know if that's what we're looking for," he said, "but I also don't think we can take the word of a driver."

"Well, whose word would you take?"

"Did you bring that gorgeous horse of yours with you?" Pike asked.

"I did," Clint said. "He's in the hotel's stable."

"What would you think about taking a ride out there and having a look yourself?"

"Why would you take my word?"

"I'd take your word over that of a driver," Pike said.

Clint paused a moment, then said, "Now that you mention it, I was thinking about doing that myself. Eclipse could use the exercise."

"So you'll do it?"

"Why not?" Clint asked. "I should be able to tell if a dam is crumbling or not."

"And meet me here again tomorrow?"

Clint sat back in his chair and looked around.

"What is it?" Pike asked.

"I'm still wondering what's supposed to be wrong with this place," Clint said. "Why that cab driver was so reluctant to take me here."

Pike shrugged and said, "You got me. Look, why don't you meet me out front tomorrow and then we'll go someplace, have lunch, and you can tell me what you found out there."

"Okay," Clint said. "I'll go over to the stable now and saddle Eclipse. He'll be happy to get out and stretch those big legs."

"I wish I could ride out there with you," Pike said, "but

I'm trying to keep a low profile until I finally know exactly what I have to do."

"That's okay," Clint said. "I understand."

"What about that woman who came to your room?" Pike asked. "Have you seen her again?"

"No," Clint said. "I spent most of my time out at the club yesterday, and there are no women there at all."

"No, there wouldn't be," Pike said. "It's definitely men only."

"I find that very easy to believe."

EIGHTEEN

Clint entered the hotel's stable and found Eclipse standing quietly in his stall.

"How you doing, big fella?" he asked, slapping the big Darley Arabian on the hip.

Eclipse turned his head and stared at Clint balefully.

"Yeah, yeah, I know you're glad to see me," Clint said. "Come on, we're going for a little ride."

He backed the horse out of his stall and saddled him, then walked him out and mounted up.

"Let's go!" he said, and kicked him into a run.

When they got well out of town, Clint really let the horse stretch his legs. It was invigorating, for him and the horse, to let the animal run this way.

He followed the route that Jason had taken both times when driving Clint out to the club and back. Clint had kept a sharp eye out the window so that he'd know the way.

Dash Charles, the engineer, with his two colleagues, Kevin Dale and Frank Conlin, examined the face of the dam, occasionally poking at it with a steel pike.

"This is the third place we've looked," Conlin said. "I don't notice anything."

"That's because you don't know what you're lookin' at," Charles said. "Come here."

Conlin approached the point of the dam that Dash Charles was standing in front of.

"What?"

"Poke it."

"What?"

"Poke it with your finger."

Conlin poked.

"Harder."

Conlin did it.

"Come on, harder."

Conlin poked again, harder this time, and his finger went into the wall.

"Hey," he said, "like the kid with the dike."

"Yeah, well," Dash Charles said, "that's not supposed to happen."

Conlin pulled his finger out.

"It happened in the other two places we looked as well," Charles said.

"So what are we supposed to do?" Kevin Dale asked.

"I have to let the club know," Charles said. "And they have to hire somebody to come out and fix it."

"So? Do it," Dale said.

"This is going to be an expensive fix," Charles said.

"So?"

"So that won't make them happy," the engineer said.

"But they gotta do it, right?" Conlin asked.

"Yes, they do," Charles said, "if I tell them about it."

"Why wouldn't you?" Dale asked.

"Because they might fire me."

"So what are you gonna do?" Conlin asked.

"I don't know," Charles said. "I'll see if I can figure out a cheaper way to fix it before I tell them anything."

"Why would they fire you?" Conlin asked.

"Because I was specifically asked to find a cheap fix," Charles said. "If I don't, and they have to spend more money, they'll just stop paying me."

"Hey," Conlin said, "if you stop gettin' paid, we stop gettin' paid."

"That's right."

"Jesus," Conlin said, "we don't want that to happen."

Charles and Dale stared at him.

Clint looked down at the three men standing in front of the dam. He was high on a bluff. They'd see him if they bothered to look up, but at the moment, their entire focus was on the dam. One man even seemed to be poking it. Clint wished he had a long glass so he could take a better look.

The three men walked along the dam, one man paying more attention than the others. It was possible that these were engineers working for the club. He decided to find himself another stretch of dam that he could examine on his own.

He turned Eclipse and rode away, still without having been seen.

"Did you see that?" Dale asked.

"What?" Dash Charles asked. Conlin looked at Dale as well. Dale was looking upward.

"I thought I saw someone up on that bluff," Dale said.

"Doing what?"

"I'm not sure," Dale said. "Maybe he was watching us."

"He?"

"Well, what would a girl be doin' up there?"

Charles looked up.

"Nobody there now."

"No," Dale said, "I think he—whoever it was—was riding away."

Charles looked at Dale, then at Conlin.

"Okay," he said, "let's finish up here and take a look up there."

NINETEEN

Clint rode Eclipse up to the dam wall and dismounted. He dropped Eclipse's reins to the ground and walked to the wall. It towered over him as he went along, dragging his hand over it. He didn't know why he had agreed to do this. He wasn't an engineer. The dam—right here anyway—looked fine. Then again, those other three men seemed to be examining it very closely.

He decided to ride back to where he had seen them. If they were gone, he'd try to figure out what they had discovered.

On the top of the bluff, Dash Charles dismounted and studied the ground.

"One rider. Looks like you were right, Kevin," he said to Dale.

"But that doesn't mean he was watchin' us," Conlin said.

"Why else would he be up here?"

Conlin shrugged. "Maybe he was just takin' a ride, or wanted to get a look at the dam."

"I can't accept that," Charles said.

"So what do we do?" Dale asked.

"We keep doin' our job," Charles said, "but keep a sharp eye out for anybody watching us."

He mounted up again.

"Come on, we still have things to look at."

As Jason, the driver, entered the lounge, Henry Clay Frick lowered his newspaper and looked up at the man.

"Yes, Jason?"

"I have something to tell you, sir."

There were two other members in the room, each sitting alone and reading a newspaper. They didn't seem to be listening, but it was difficult to have a private conversation in that room.

"What is it, Jason?"

"When I brought Mr. Adams back to his hotel last night, he asked me a lot of questions."

"Is that so?"

"He invited me to have a drink, and then bought me several mugs of beer."

Frick frowned.

"He was trying to get you drunk, do you think?" he asked the driver.

"Well," Jason said, "let's say he was trying to loosen my lips."

"And did he?"

"Let me tell you what we talked about."

Frick listened attentively as Jason related the conversation to him.

"I see," he finally said.

"I hope I didn't speak out of turn, sir."

"No, Jason," Flick said. "You did fine. Thank you for telling me."

"Yes, sir," Jason said, and left. As he did, the other two men lowered their newspapers. They were Evan Lawrence and William Bledsoe. Both men set their newspapers aside, stood, and approached Frick.

"Adams is asking questions," Bledsoe said.

"He wouldn't be who he is if he didn't," Frick said.

"Yes, but maybe he's asking too many, Henry," Lawrence said.

"I don't think so," Frick said. "Besides, I think I can handle whatever questions he has."

Lawrence and Bledsoe exchanged a glance.

"Yes," Frick said, "I know, we need to talk to the others. But I think they'll go along with me."

"I hope you're right," Lawrence said.

The three gentlemen went back to their individual chairs and newspapers.

Clint saw the three men on the bluff, and knew they had spotted him there earlier. One of them studied the ground, then mounted, and the three of them rode off, two of them looking around. Clint, however, was well hidden and remained unseen.

Once the three men were gone, he rode down to the dam, where he had previously seen them. He hurriedly dismounted and studied the wall. Here—unlike the previous part of the wall he'd examined—he could see chips in the armor. He also saw some holes, which he assumed the man with the pike had caused.

In places, the wall seemed to be flaking. He wasn't an engineer, but he knew that shoring up this wall would be an expensive proposition for the club. Rich men being rich men, they would not look forward to spending that money.

But what did their invitation to come visit the club have

to do with the dam? And what did the dam have to do with Jeremy Pike being there?

He mounted Eclipse and rode away. He had enough to talk with Pike about at lunch the next day. He headed back to Pittsburgh.

TWENTY

Back in the city, he returned Eclipse to the hotel stable, where he unsaddled him and rubbed him down himself before returning to the hotel.

"Mr. Adams!" the clerk called as he entered.

"Yes?"

"You have a message, sir."

Clint walked to the desk and accepted a slip of paper from Steve.

"Who dropped it off?" he asked.

"A woman."

"Brown hair, kind of mousy?"

"No, sir," Steve said, "quite attractive."

Clint considered taking the message to his room to read, but instead opened it right away. It said: MEET ME AT THE KEYSTONE RESTAURANT AT SEVEN. IT'S IMPORTANT. It was signed "L," which he assumed meant Lizzie.

"Where's the Keystone Restaurant?" Clint asked Steve.

"A few blocks away, sir," Steve said. "It's very high-end, but excellent."

"Okay," Clint said. "Thank you."

He went to his room.

He stood at the window of his room and looked down at the street while he considered his course of action. Did Lizzie know that he was aware that she did not work with Jeremy Pike? Was she planning to try to continue that ruse? Or was she ready to reveal to him who she really was, and what she wanted?

Or was this some kind of trap?

He had been wearing his Colt in his holster while in Pittsburgh, and to date no one had come up to him to tell him he couldn't. If he was in New York, or San Francisco, or Denver, he might have left the holster in his room and carried the little Colt New Line he often used as a hideaway. But not knowing what was waiting for him at the Keystone, he wore the holster when he left the room. And he had the New Line tucked into his belt at the small of his back.

The Keystone turned out to be close enough to walk. As he made the trip, he paid attention to his back trail, but did not feel that anyone was tailing him. That was good.

When he reached the restaurant, he saw what Steve had meant about it being high-end. The plate glass windows were etched with gold lettering, and there was a white-gloved doorman out in front. He was glad he had worn his new clothes, even though they still did not fit the venue.

"Sir," the doorman said, "you cannot enter while wearing that gun."

Restaurant policy, he wondered, or an attempt to disarm him?

"I have a meeting inside with a lady," Clint said.

"If you're meeting a lady, sir," the big doorman said, "you shouldn't need a gun. I can hold it for you."

"I'm afraid not."

"Then I'm afraid you can't go in."

"Is your manager or owner available?"

"Sure thing," the doorman said, "but that's not going to help you."

"Just get him."

"The owner," the doorman said, "is a lady, sir. Mrs. Denham."

"Fine," Clint said, "I'll talk to Mrs. Denham, then."

"As you wish," the man said. "Wait here."

The doorman went inside, leaving Clint alone. He felt as if he had a target painted on his back. But in studying the street on his side, and across the street, he did not see anyone paying special attention to him. He scanned the rooftops across the way, and still saw nothing.

The doorman reappeared with a lady in an emerald green dress that revealed her smooth shoulders. She had long red hair and green eyes.

"Is there a problem, sir?"

"Yes," Clint said, "I'd like to come into your restaurant. I'm meeting a lady."

"I don't see a problem there," she said. "All you have to do is leave your gun with Winston here."

"Winston told me that," Clint said, "but I explained to him that I can't do that."

"Sir," she said, "we simply cannot allow you inside while you're wearing that gun."

"And I can't take it off."

"Well," she said, "perhaps I can talk to your dining companion and ask her to come out, and then the two of you can go somewhere else."

"That's fine," Clint said. "I'm meeting a woman named Lizzie."

"What does she look like?"

"She's . . . kind of statuesque, very attractive . . . I don't know what she's wearing."

"I'll do my best to find her," the woman said, and went back inside, leaving Clint and the doorman, Winston, to glare at each other.

When the woman returned to the door several minutes later, she was alone. She also had an odd look on her face.

"Mrs. Denham?" Winston said.

"It's all right, Winston," she said. "Mr. Adams can come inside."

"Adams?" Winston asked.

"Yes," she said, "Clint Adams."

Winston looked at Clint.

"The Gunsmith?"

"Yes," Mrs. Denham said, "the Gunsmith." She looked at Clint. "Follow me, please."

"Thank you."

They stepped into the restaurant, and then Mrs. Denham stopped short.

"Why didn't you tell us who you are?" she asked.

"I didn't know if it would make a difference," he said. "Besides, I don't like announcing myself."

"Well, come this way," she said, "I'll take you to Miss Livingston's table."

As he followed her, he thought, Lizzie Livingston?

TWENTY-ONE

As they approached Miss Livingston's table, Clint hardly recognized the woman seated there.

"Miss Livingston," Mrs. Denham said, "your guest has arrived."

"Thank you, Shannon."

"I'll have your waiter come right over."

Shannon Denham actually held Clint's chair for him, then went off to find their waiter.

He stared across the table at the woman who looked nothing like "Lizzie."

"So I guess your name's not Lizzie," he said.

"No."

"And you don't work with or for Jeremy Pike."

A small smile touched her mouth and she said, "No."

"Then I suppose you've invited me here to tell me the truth?"

She didn't answer right away.

"Or some version of the truth," he added.

She smiled fully now.

"All right," she said. "First, my name is Elizabeth Livingston."

"So your name really is Lizzie Livingston?"

"My friends call me Beth."

"Well," Clint said, "that sounds a little better."

Her auburn hair was expertly piled atop her head, revealing a long, graceful neck. She was wearing a red gown, which showed just a shadowy hint of her cleavage— enough to interest any man. She did not resemble in the least the "whore" Lizzie. She had makeup on, but nothing like the heavy face paint she'd worn as Lizzie.

"You clean up pretty well," she said. "I see you bought new clothes."

"I didn't know I'd be eating in a place like this, though," he said, "or I would have bought a new suit."

"You look fine," she said, "and the meal is on me."

"How did Mrs. Denham find you?" he asked. "You don't much match the description I gave her."

"Shannon and I are friends."

"But you didn't tell her who I was?"

"Not until she asked," Beth said. "I thought it would be . . . fun. I see you got in with your gun still on."

"Yes."

A waiter came over and said, "I'm Albert, ma'am. May I take your order?" He was a small, sparse-haired man with a white shirt and black bow tie.

"May I?" she asked, looking at Clint.

"Please," he said. "I assume you've been here before."

"Well," she said, "you look like a steak man, so the gentleman will have a steak dinner, and I will have the roast chicken."

"Yes, ma'am."

"And two beers," she said.

The waiter nodded and said, "Right away."

"So I assume you've seen Pike and he's told you he doesn't know me," she said.

"Oh, yes."

"Well," she said, "I don't want to say he lied to you. Maybe if you were able to describe me in a different way, he would have guessed."

"So you two do know each other?"

"I would say we're kind of rivals."

"Wait," Clint said, "he works for the government. Do you also work for the government, but in another branch?"

"Let's just say that very often, our interests . . . intersect."

"So I'm not getting the whole truth out of you tonight," Clint said.

"I'm afraid not."

"Okay," Clint said, "I suppose I'll have to take what I can get."

The waiter returned with two mugs of ice-cold beer.

"Cheers," she said. They clinked glasses and drank. "Why don't we eat dinner, and then we can talk over dessert."

"That works for me . . . Beth."

The steak dinner was excellent. The meat itself was cooked perfectly, with plenty of blood on the plate. The potatoes, onions, and carrots were all steamed to perfection.

Beth had an entire roast chicken on her plate, and attacked it and the vegetables with the same gusto she'd exhibited in his room.

When both of their plates were decimated, the waiter came over and cleared the table.

"Mr. Adams will have some peach pie," she told him, "and I'll have cherry. And coffee."

"Yes, ma'am."

"And make the coffee very strong."

"As you wish, ma'am."

He walked away, and Clint and Beth regarded each other across the table.

"How did you know I like peach pie?"

"I did my research."

"Before or after we spent the night together?"

She just smiled.

TWENTY-TWO

The waiter brought the pie and the coffee, and it was just as good as the rest of the meal.

"So tell me," Clint said around his last bite of pie, "why did you choose to come clean with me tonight . . . sort of?"

"Well, you've talked with Pike," she said, "and you've talked with Henry Frick and some of his colleagues. I guess I figured you've been lied to enough."

"And, of course," he said, "you're not going to lie to me."

"Not anymore," she said.

Clint had the feeling it wasn't going to be any less either.

"I saw that you took a ride today."

If she actually "saw" him ride out that afternoon, he was impressed because he hadn't seen her.

"My horse needed to stretch his legs."

"And that's all?" she asked. "You didn't ride out to take a look at the dam?"

If she'd followed him out to the dam, he was now annoyed with himself. But she could have been guessing.

"Why would I do that?" he asked. "I don't know anything about dams."

She abruptly changed the subject.

"Do you know a man named Dash Charles?"

"Dash?"

"Believe it or not," she said, "his mother and father named him Dashmore."

"Sounds like somebody who would be in a foul mood a lot," he commented.

"Not quite," she said. "He's an engineer, but he's also quite good with a gun."

"He's multitalented, then."

"Oh yes," she said, and he had the feeling she wasn't referring to either of the talents she'd already mentioned.

"So I guess you're going to tell me he's working as an engineer for the club?"

"Exactly."

"And the gun?"

"He'll use that, too, if he has to. He also has two men working with him."

Three men, he thought. Like the three men he'd seen out at the dam.

"Do you know who they are?"

"Locals," she said. "Not much talent between them. Dale and Conlin."

He nodded.

"Did you see them out there today? While you were stretching your horse's legs?"

He realized that he was getting nothing out of Beth Livingston, maybe not even her real name. She had invited him here to pump him for what he knew.

"Not me," he said. "It was just me and my horse out there."

"I see."

"Beth," Clint said, "I enjoyed this meal, but if you've got nothing else to give me, I'm going to head back to my hotel."

"Clint," she asked, "didn't our night together mean anything to you?"

"What do you want from me, Beth?" he asked.

"I want to know what Jeremy Pike is doing in Pittsburgh," she admitted.

"Why don't you ask him?"

"Like I said," she answered, "we're rivals."

"Then I'm afraid I can't help you," he said—mainly because he himself wasn't sure what Jeremy was doing in Pittsburgh.

"Clint—"

"Beth," he said, standing up, "good night, and thank you."

"Won't you even walk me back to my hotel?"

"I'll bet you have transportation."

"Then I'll take you back to your hotel."

"I can walk."

"But . . . I could stay the night?"

"I'm a little tired," he said.

She looked frustrated with him.

"Don't be a sonofabitch, Clint Adams!"

"Beth—or whatever your real name is—it was a lovely meal. Thank you so much."

He headed for the door, feeling very satisfied with himself. He'd enjoyed his time with her in bed, and wouldn't have minded another go-round—but not tonight. On this night it was more satisfying to leave her there, feeling frustrated.

Clint had just left the restaurant when Winston, the doorman, called out, "Sir?"

"I don't need a cab," he told the big man. "I'll walk."

"It's not that, sir," Winston said. "Mrs. Denham would like a moment of your time, if you're willing."

"Sure," Clint said after only the briefest consideration, "why not?"

TWENTY-THREE

Instead of taking him back into the building, Winston walked Clint down the street to another door and held it open for him. As Clint entered, he found himself in another dining room, this one empty except for Shannon Denham, who was seated at a table.

"Mr. Adams," she said, "thank you for agreeing to see me. Brandy?"

Why was everybody in Pittsburgh offering him brandy?

"Sure."

She had a decanter and two snifters on the table before her. She poured some into both.

"Join me?" she asked.

He walked to the table and sat down. She pushed one of the snifters across to him.

"Let me get right to the point," she said.

"That would be refreshing."

"I want to be the first woman to join the South Fork Fishing and Hunting Club."

"Uh-huh."

"And I'd like you to help me."

"What makes you think I can do that?"

"Well . . . you're the Gunsmith. They'd love to have you as a member."

"Do you think so?"

"Haven't you been out there?" she asked. "Haven't you been invited?"

"I have not." He sipped the brandy. He supposed it was good, but he still preferred beer.

"You haven't been out there, or haven't been invited?" she asked.

"What's the difference?" Clint asked. "I can't help you, Mrs. Denham."

"Shannon," she said. "Just call me Shannon. Can I ask you something else?"

"Go ahead."

"Are you and Beth . . . a couple?"

"No," he said.

"You answered very quickly."

"I've only known her a few days."

"I see."

"Is there anything else?"

"You keep staring at me."

"Well," he said, "you're very beautiful."

"Why . . . thank you."

He stood up, and she followed.

"I invite you to eat here again, Mr. Adams, anytime you like."

"The food was excellent," Clint said. "Your prices are a bit high, though."

"That's not a problem," she said. "You would dine as my guest. Anytime."

"I appreciate that," Clint said, "but as I said, I really can't do anything for you regarding the hunting club."

"Oh, I understand," she said, "but somebody in this

town has to break up that boys' club. You see, I have the wealth to match up with some of them. And the position. I'm just the wrong . . . sex."

"It seems to me even if you did become a member, they wouldn't treat you very well. Why would you want to subject yourself to that?"

"Because it has to be done, Mr. Adams," she said. "It simply has to be done. Would you like me to have Winston get you a cab?"

"No, thanks," Clint said. "I walked here, and I can walk back. Thanks for the drink."

"Good night, Mr. Adams."

"Clint," he said, "Just call me Clint . . . Shannon."

TWENTY-FOUR

The next day Jeremy Pike was standing outside Solomon's Saloon when Clint arrived.

"Clint," he said, shaking hands, "good to see you. There's a place down the street."

"Lead the way." As they walked, Clint said, "I had an interesting dinner last night."

"Oh? Where?"

"A place called the Keystone."

"Ouch," Pike said. "That's expensive. Who was footing the bill for that?"

"A woman named Beth Livingston."

Pike stopped short and looked at him.

"Beth?"

"Yep."

"She's here in Pittsburgh?"

"Not only that," Clint said. "She was Lizzie."

"The whore?"

Clint nodded.

"I knew she was a bitch, but not a whore." Pike shook his head. "Come on."

* * *

Pike took Clint to a small café on a street corner, many, many levels beneath the Keystone.

"Not fancy," Pike said, "but the food's good."

They went inside and got a table easily, since the place was empty.

They both ordered bowls of beef stew for lunch, and mugs of beer.

"Okay," Clint said, "tell me about Beth Livingston."

"She used to be with the Secret Service."

"Used to be?"

"She left after a few years, frustrated that she wasn't being given important assignments."

"So what did she do?"

"She tried to join the Pinkertons, but they wouldn't have her."

"And?"

"She struck out on her own."

"So she's a private detective?"

"Not exactly," he said.

"What does that mean?"

"She doesn't have a license, but from time to time she does that kind of work."

"And the other times?"

"She tries to horn in on Secret Service business."

"And that's what she's doing now."

"Is she?"

"Well, she's been trying to get information out of me, while she has nothing to give me."

"You didn't tell her anything, did you?"

"No," Clint said, "not a thing."

The waiter brought their bowls, and a basket of biscuits.

"But I met another interesting woman."

"Who's that?"

"Shannon Denham."

"Again," Pike said, "who's that?"

"She owns the Keystone," Clint said. "And she asked me to help her break the ban on women joining the South Fork Fishing and Hunting Club."

"What?"

"She said that someone has to do it."

"Why would she think you can help her?"

"Because I have a reputation," Clint said. "She thinks they'll ask me to join."

"And she's right, isn't she?" Pike asked. "Have they asked?"

"Not yet."

"All right," Pike said, "let's move on. Did you ride out to the dam?"

"I did."

"And?"

"I saw three other men out there, examining a portion of the dam."

"Who were they?"

"From what Beth told me, one of them was probably a man named Dash Charles."

"Charles," Pike said. "He's an odd one."

"What's so odd?"

"He's educated as an engineer, but he also makes his way with a gun. He's probably working for the club in one capacity or the other."

"Or both. Anyway, I took a look at portions of the dam, didn't know what I was looking at until I looked at the same section I saw him looking at."

"And?"

"It needs work."

"Plugging?"

"Shoring up," Clint said. "The expensive kind, I'm sure. And it's up to the club to see it gets done. If that dam goes, everything in its path will be destroyed."

"Jesus," Pike said, "Johnstown would be right in that path."

TWENTY-FIVE

They finished their stew, nursed another beer each.

"So?" Clint said. "Is this what you wanted? Information about the dam?"

"Not sure," Pike said. "Could be."

"You know, I asked Beth why she chose last night to reveal herself to me," Clint said. "Do you know what she said?"

"What?"

"She thought I'd been lied to enough by everyone I've been talking to."

"Including me?"

"That was the insinuation."

"I haven't lied about anything, Clint," Pike said. "I just don't know what we've got. Will you be going to the club again?"

"The only reason I'd have to do that would be if I was going to apply for membership."

"Or if they were going to invite you."

"Yes."

"Do you think they will?"

"Probably."

"Good—uh, but will you go?"

"I don't know, Jeremy."

"What do you mean?" Pike asked.

"I'm still operating in the dark, Jeremy," Clint said. "I don't like operating in the dark."

"And yet you have been doing quite well."

"Have I?"

"The club members like you, they're probably going to ask you to join, and you've seen the dam."

"I'm confused about one thing."

"What's that?"

"Why would they ask me to join?" Clint said. "I don't live here—in Pittsburgh, or in South Fork."

"A lot of them don't either," Pike said, "but that's apparently okay. As long as you have the money for membership, you don't need to live near here. They're all rich men. They can get here anytime they want to."

"Well, I'm not rich."

"That doesn't matter," Pike said. "If you're invited, you don't have to pay."

"If I accept."

"True."

"And you want me to."

"Please."

Clint sat back and took a deep breath.

"This is crazy. I usually like to know what I'm doing, and why . . . but okay. If they invite me, I'll accept."

"Thank you," Pike said, "and once you're a member, you'll be able to get an even closer look at what's going on up there."

"Whatever it is," Clint said.

"I'll pay the check," Pike said.

* * *

They stepped outside and stopped.

"Now what?" Clint asked.

"What do you mean?"

"I mean, when do we meet again?"

"I guess when you have something to tell me."

"Or," Clint said, "when you have something to tell me, right?"

Pike didn't answer.

"I mean," Clint said, "you are working while you're here, right? You're not just sitting around waiting for me to find something . . . are you?"

"No, of course not. You're right. If I find out something, I'll get in touch."

"And how do I get in touch with you?"

"Solomon's," Pike said. "Leave word there, and I'll get back to you."

"Pike—"

"Just work on this a little longer for me, Clint," Pike said. "I know we're close."

Pike turned and walked away as Clint said to himself, "But close to what?"

TWENTY-SIX

"Clint Adams," the well-dressed man said.

"What?" Dash Charles asked.

"It had to be Clint Adams," the man said, "the man you said was watching you."

"Clint Adams is here? In Pittsburgh?"

"Yes," the other man said. "Henry Frick brought him to the club."

"Why didn't you tell me?"

"It's not your business," the man said. "The dam is your business. What have you found out?"

"Wait a minute," Charles said. "Go back to Clint Adams. Why did Frick bring him to the club?"

"He wants us to vote him in as a member."

"And are you going to?"

"I don't know," the man said. "That's not important. The dam is important."

"The dam needs to be repaired," Charles said, "in more than one place."

"Can it be done cheaply?"

"I don't know," Charles replied. "I'm still thinking about that."

He looked around. They were meeting in the same low-rent saloon, but today they and the bartender were the only ones there.

"You better find a way to fix it, then," the man said. "That's what I'm paying you for."

"Well, if Clint Adams is here, that changes things."

"Why? How?"

"Because of my other profession. The one where I use my gun. That puts me right on a collision course with him."

"It doesn't have to."

"Yes, it does. He has one of the biggest reputations in the West with a gun. Maybe the biggest. You know what that means?"

"This is not the Wild West, Charles," the man said. "This is Pittsburgh. This is a civilized city."

"Is it? Have you read the papers lately?" Charles asked. "Three people have been killed in the past few days. How damn civilized is that?"

"Dash—"

"If I kill Clint Adams," Dash Charles said, "I won't need your money anymore."

When Clint got back to his hotel, he found a man waiting for him in the lobby. He was tall, with brown hair going gray at the temples, wearing a three-piece suit that had seen better days. Clint also noticed that beneath the suit was a gun in a shoulder holster.

"Mr. Adams?" the man said.

Clint looked at the desk clerk, figuring he had somehow given the man a sign when he entered the lobby. Steve, the clerk, looked away.

"That's right."

"Sir, my name is William J. Kane," the man said. He had a bushy brown mustache and bright blue eyes. He appeared to be in his early thirties. He did not offer to shake hands.

"And?"

"Lieutenant William J. Kane," the man said, "Pittsburgh Police Department."

"What can I do for you, Lieutenant?" Clint folded his arms across his chest.

Kane's eyes went to the gun on Clint's hip. Clint had left the Colt New Line in his room that morning.

"Sir, I'll need to take your gun."

"You're here to take my gun?" Clint became aware of similarly suited men on either side of him in the lobby. They hadn't made a move toward him . . . yet. Kane and the other men were all wearing bowler hats that matched their suits.

"Yes, sir."

"Why?"

"We can't permit you to keep walking our streets wearing a gun, sir."

"I haven't broken any laws that I know of."

"Well, you did recently enter an establishment that required you to give up your firearm, and you did not comply."

"I had permission from the owner."

"Is that a fact?" Kane asked. "Well, we can check that out. But for now, I need your gun."

"Do you know who I am?"

"I do," Kane said. "But we can't be making exceptions for every Western gunman who comes to town."

"If I give up my gun, I could be dead in a matter of minutes."

"Oh, I think you're exaggerating, sir. I don't think there

are men in Pittsburgh just waiting for you to be disarmed so they can kill you."

"Why am I not as sure about that as you are?"

"Sir, your gun."

"I'm not giving it up."

"Then we will have to take it." Kane made a hand signal and the other policemen—three of them—moved closer. "If you fail to comply, I'll have to arrest you and put you in a cell."

"And I'll probably be safer there," Clint said.

"Then sir," Kane said, "I regret to inform you that you are under arrest."

The other policemen took out their guns, and Clint raised his arms.

TWENTY-SEVEN

Clint sat in a jail cell for three hours—without his gun—before a policeman came to his cell door.

"You have a visitor," the man said.

"Who?"

He didn't answer. He just stuck the key in the lock and opened the door. Another man appeared and entered.

"Clint."

"Henry."

"Don't stand," Frick said, raising his hand. Clint had no intention of rising. The policeman closed and locked the cell door behind them.

"May I sit?"

"Help yourself."

Frick sat on the cot next to him.

"I just got word that you'd been arrested."

"From who?"

"The clerk at the hotel."

"He's the one who pointed me out to the police."

"He had no choice."

"I suppose not. Can you get me out of here?"

"Maybe," Frick said. "You haven't broken any serious laws that I know of."

"None at all."

"But it seems there have been some murders in Pittsburgh over the past three days."

"And? What's that got to do with me?"

"The police just want to question you about them."

"They think I did these killings?"

"Well," Frick said, "they've only happened since you came to town."

"Coincidence." Clint hated that word.

"Undoubtedly," Frick said, "but I told them you'd answer their questions."

"Sure, why not? And then I go free?"

"Yes."

"And get my gun back?"

"Well . . ."

"Why not?"

"There is a way."

"How?"

"If you were a member of the South Fork Fishing and Hunting Club, we could give you a room at the club. If you're not in Pittsburgh, they can't take your gun."

"But I'm not a member," Clint said, "and don't your members need to vote to make me one?"

"A mere technicality," Frick said. "I'll just stretch the truth a little." He stood up and called out, "Guard!"

They took Clint to a bare room, with just a table and two chairs. Lieutenant Kane was waiting there.

"Have a seat, Mr. Adams," Kane sad. "I assume Mr. Frick is outside?"

"He is."

"Well," Kane said, "I'll try not to take too long."

Clint sat across from Kane at the table.

"I just have a few questions."

"Go ahead . . ."

Kane questioned him about the three people who had been killed—two men and a woman. Clint answered the questions honestly. He'd never heard of any of them.

"How were they killed?"

"Why does that matter?" Kane asked. "I mean, if you don't know them?"

"I'm assuming they were shot," Clint said, "or you wouldn't be questioning me."

"Well, yes, they were shot."

"Do you have other suspects?"

"We have some," Kane said. "I'll be questioning them, just as I've questioned you."

"Am I free to go?"

"For now."

"I'll need my gun."

Kane hesitated, then opened a drawer, and took out the gun and holster.

"Of course," he said, "although it goes against my better judgment."

Clint accepted the gun and holster, stood up, and strapped them on.

"I imagine you felt naked without that."

"Very," Clint said.

"That must be a difficult way to live."

"It's the only way I know," Clint said.

Kane stood up and opened the door of the room.

"An officer will show you the way out," he said.

Clint stepped out of the room, into the hall, where a uniformed officer was waiting.

"Where's Mr. Frick?"

"He's outside the building, sir."

"Well then," Clint said, "lead the way."

TWENTY-EIGHT

Frick was indeed waiting out front for Clint, with Jason and the carriage.

"Ready to go?" Frick asked.

"We've got to stop at my hotel first."

"No problem."

Jason held the door open for both of them, then climbed aboard and got under way.

"I have a question," Clint said.

"I thought you might," Frick replied.

"Did you have anything to do with me being arrested?" Clint asked.

"Why would I do that?"

"So you could offer me sanctuary at the club."

"That would have been a good idea," Frick said, "but no, I did not. I was quite surprised when I received word that you had been arrested."

"I don't suppose they really suspected me of any of those murders."

"I suspect," Frick said, "that they simply took advantage of the situation to ask you some questions."

"You're probably right."

They rode the rest of the way in silence.

Frick waited outside while Clint packed his carpetbag and checked out of his hotel.

"It was a pleasure to have you, Mr. Adams," Steve, the clerk, said.

Clint didn't respond as he paid his bill.

"Sir," the clerk said, "about the police—"

"I know," Clint said, "you had no choice."

"No, sir."

"And I suppose I should thank you for contacting Mr. Frick about my arrest."

"Well . . . I felt it was the right thing to do, sir."

"It probably was," Clint said, "and I'm sure Mr. Frick has taken care of you for it."

"Oh, yes, sir."

"I'm going to leave my horse here for a while," Clint said. "That animal is the most important thing to me, so if anything happens to him, I'll hold you personally responsible."

The clerk swallowed, his eyes wide, and said, "You can count on me, sir."

Clint had to send a message to Pike at Solomon's Saloon, but he didn't know if he should trust the task to the clerk or not. Chances were he'd tell Frick about it. But who else could he depend on to send such a message?

He looked around the lobby, saw several bellboys, and the doorman standing at the door.

"Anyway . . . thanks," he said, and walked to the door.

"Sir," the doorman said.

"I need to send a message," Clint said, "without the clerk knowing about it."

"He is a bit shiftless, sir."

"Can I trust you to send it?"

"I can handle that job, sir."

"Okay," Clint said. "I'll be right back."

He went back inside, asked a bellman for a piece of paper and a pencil. He wrote as simple a message as he could to let Pike know what was happening, then carried it outside and handed it to the doorman with a few silver dollars.

"Thank you, sir. I'll see that it's delivered as soon as possible."

"Thanks."

Clint walked down to the street, where the carriage was still waiting, Jason standing alongside it.

"Ready to go, sir?"

"I'm ready, Jason."

Jason took his bag and held the door for him. Clint heard the man climb aboard, and secure the carpetbag on top. Then he remained silent and still, waiting for instructions.

Inside, Frick said, "You seemed bothered."

"My horse," Clint said. "I'm having second thoughts about leaving him here."

"Well, then, there's no need to," Frick said. He knocked on the top of the carriage.

"Jason, pull around to the hotel stable."

Clint went into the stable, and walked Eclipse out after putting his bridle on. As he tied the reins to the back of the carriage, Jason went inside and came out carrying the saddle, which he secured to the top.

When Clint got back to the carriage with Frick, he said, "Thank you for that."

"We have an excellent stable at the club, and several

handlers who know what they're doing. Your magnificent horse will be in good hands."

"That makes me feel a lot better."

Frick knocked on the roof of the carriage and Jason got them under way.

TWENTY-NINE

The meeting this time between Dash Charles and his employer was hurriedly arranged, and took place on a street corner.

As the well-dressed man approached, Charles could see how unhappy he was. His bodyguard followed right behind him.

"I don't like these rushed meetings," he complained.

"Hey," Charles said, "you called it."

"I know," the man said, "but only because you are being so unreasonable about this Gunsmith thing."

"This is about the Gunsmith?"

"I'm afraid so."

"Well, what is it?"

"He was arrested earlier today."

"For what?"

"It doesn't matter," the man said. "He's out. Frick got him out and has offered him sanctuary at the club."

"Sanctuary?"

"The police won't touch him there."

"What the hell did they want him for?"

"Essentially," the man said, "as I understand it, they were attempting to disarm him."

"Christ," Charles said, "killing an unarmed Gunsmith would get me nothing."

"Well, you don't have to worry about that," the man said. "He's been released, and they gave him his gun back. But he's left his hotel and is on his way to the club."

Charles rubbed his jaw.

"That might actually be better for me," he said. "I'd be out of place in his hotel, but I have the right to be at the club, since I'm the engineer for the dam."

"Oh my God, you're not going to kill him at the club, are you?"

"What are their plans for him?"

"What are the usual plans for someone like the Gunsmith—although we've never really had someone of his caliber there."

"I want the first shot at him," Charles said.

"I wish you'd just be satisfied to do your job," the man said. "Look, I'll increase you salary by half."

"My salary is fine," Charles said. He looked past his employer at the bodyguard, who stood by silently, seemingly staring at nothing in particular.

"How come he never speaks?" he asked.

"Because *he* knows his job," the man said, "and speaking isn't part of it."

The bodyguard's eyes did not flinch.

"I have to go," the man said, looking around uncomfortably.

"Go ahead," Charles said. "I'll be coming out to the club soon."

"Why?"

"Just tell your colleagues that we're meeting about the dam," the engineer said.

"And will we?"

"Yes," Charles said. "I'll have a solution by then."

"You'd better," the man said. "For the money we're paying you—"

"Hey," Charles said, cutting him off, "didn't I just save you money by not taking you up on a salary increase? You know, for some of us, life is about more than money."

The man blinked, stared at him, and said, "I don't understand."

Charles turned and walked away.

He found his two friends, Dale and Conlin, waiting in the dive saloon they were using as a meeting place. He got himself a beer and joined them at their table. Counting the three of them, there were six people in the saloon.

"You look bothered," Dale said.

"The opposite," Charles said. "Turns out the Gunsmith left his hotel and went to the club."

"And that's good?" Conlin asked.

"Yeah, it is," Charles said. "I can deal with the Gunsmith out there without having to worry about the police."

"Yeah, but can we come out there?" Dale asked.

"We'll work it out," Charles said.

"Why'd he move?" Conlin asked.

"He got arrested," Charles said. "Seems the police wanted to disarm him."

"That woulda made him easier to take," Conlin said.

Dash Charles stared at him.

"What good does it do me to kill an unarmed Gunsmith?" he demanded.

"Well," Conlin said, "at least that way he wouldn't be able to kill you."

"You're an idiot," Charles said.

"Yeah," Dale agreed. He looked at Charles. "So when do we go?"

"Probably tomorrow," Charles said. "I'm still working on the dam problem."

"You ain't solved that yet?" Dale asked.

"I've come up with a way to shore up the dam," Charles said, "but I don't know how long it'll hold."

"Long enough for us to get paid and get away from here?" Dale asked. "That's all we need."

"Yeah . . ." Charles said. "Yeah, that's all we need."

THIRTY

When they reached the club, Clint made a point of seeing to Eclipse's care before allowing himself to be shown to his room.

There were three handlers employed by the club, and they were all excited when Clint walked Eclipse into the stable with Jason carrying the saddle.

He discussed the Darley Arabian's care with the three men—who all seemed to be experienced—then followed Jason back to the main building. The big driver insisted on carrying the carpetbag.

"Do you have a room here, Jason?" Clint asked.

"I have a small room that I use when I stay over," Jason said.

"How often do you stay?"

"That usually depends on the members and how early they'll need me the next day."

"What goes on here at night?"

"Nothing much, sir," Jason said. "The members spend a lot of time reading their newspapers—usually the financial pages—having dinner, smoking cigars, and drinking brandy. Oh, and occasionally there is a poker game."

"Ah," Clint said, "that's the part I'm interested in. I figure I might as well make some money while I'm here. Are they any good?"

"I'm sure I don't know, sir," Jason said. "I do not know the game myself."

"So what do you do, then?"

"I read."

"Ah, so do I," Clint said.

That surprised the big man, and he raised his eyebrows.

"You? Read books?"

"I do."

"Who do you read?"

"I spend a lot of time on Twain and Dickens," Clint said. "I enjoy Dickens very much, and I enjoy Twain even more because I know him."

"You have met Mark Twain?"

"I'm proud to say we're friends," Clint said.

That changed Jason's demeanor drastically, and suddenly he became very chatty, wanting to know everything Clint knew about Mark Twain.

The two were still talking about it as they entered the building. Henry Frick was waiting there with another man, and seemed very surprised to see the two men talking.

"What's this?" he asked. "Have you two gentlemen found common ground?"

"We have," Clint said. "Literature."

"Indeed?" Frick said. Clint didn't know what surprised him more, that Jason could discuss literature, or that the Gunsmith could.

"Yes," Clint said, "indeed."

•

"Well," Frick said, indicating the Mexican-looking man standing next to him, "this is Hector. He is one of our housemen, and will show you to your room."

"All right," Clint said, watching his carpetbag change hands from Jason to Hector. "Thanks," he said to Jason.

"Yes, sir."

Jason withdrew, going back out the front door.

"Hector," Frick said, "after you've shown Mr. Adams to his room, please bring him to lounge number three."

"Yes, sir."

To Clint, he said, "Several of our members would like to have a drink with you and welcome you."

"That's fine," Clint said. "Thanks."

"This way, sir," Hector said, leading Clint to the stairway.

Clint followed Hector to the second floor, and down a long hallway of doors to one that was closed.

"This will be your room, sir," Hector said, and opened the door.

Clint entered and found himself in a larger room than he'd ever had in any hotel—including suites. It was massive. He wanted to turn to Hector and ask, "Who needs this much room?" but he didn't want to seem ungrateful.

"Is it all right, sir?" Hector asked.

"It's fine, Hector," Clint said. "More than I could ever have asked for."

"Very good, sir." He walked to the big bed and set the carpetbag down on it. "Can I show you to the lounge, sir?"

"Why don't you wait in the hall for me, Hector," Clint said. "Just a few minutes."

"As you wish, sir."

Hector left the room and closed the door behind him. Clint walked to the window and looked out. His view was of the front grounds, and he watched as Jason climbed aboard the carriage and drove it away, presumably to the stables.

He turned away from the window and went to make use of the indoor plumbing the club had.

THIRTY-ONE

Clint followed Hector back down to the first floor, then along several hallways to a lounge, where Henry Frick and some of his colleagues were waiting.

Clint recognized all the men as part of Frick's inner circle.

"Thank you, Hector," Frick said. "That'll be all."

All of the men were holding brandy glasses but there was also a waiter present, so Frick said, "Walter, please bring Mr. Adams a mug of cold beer."

"Yes, sir. Right away," the white-haired waiter said.

"Thank you," Clint said, "for not offering me a glass of brandy."

"If you become a member of the club," Frick said, "you will have at your disposal whatever beverage you might desire."

"That sounds . . . good," Clint said, wondering what would happen if he asked for a sarsaparilla.

"Have a seat," Frederick Upton said. "Anywhere."

They were all standing, leaving him a choice of any armchair he wanted. He chose one at random. When he noticed that Foster looked even more sour than usual, Clint figured he had taken the old man's favorite chair.

The rest of them seated themselves, and the waiter appeared with Clint's beer.

"Thank you," Clint said, taking it from the tray the man was holding.

The man looked slightly flustered as if he was unused to being thanked, then said, "Uh, you're welcome, sir."

"That'll be all, Walter," Frick said.

The waiter withdrew, closing the door behind him.

"Why do I have the feeling this room is only used by you gents?" Clint asked.

"That is not actually the case, but a lot of the other members do eschew the use of it."

Clint wasn't sure what "eschew" meant, but he thought he got the drift.

"Is this some sort of . . . inner circle?" Clint asked.

"Among us," Lawrence said, "we do wield a great deal of power in the club."

"Like the power to choose a new member?"

"We are actually having a meeting tomorrow to put your name forth for membership," Bledsoe said.

"So you've jumped the gun a bit by giving me a room tonight?"

"Just a little," Frick said. "But tomorrow, with the five of us voting for you, we can push it through."

"Your membership," Upton said, "is a virtual certainty."

Clint said, "Well, thank you," without feeling any gratitude.

A few miles away from the club, Dash Charles reined his horse in, causing Dale and Conlin to do the same. Even from this distance, they could see the main building.

"I always wanted to get a look inside there," Conlin commented.

"Well," Charles said, "today's not the day. This is as far as the two of you go."

"What are we supposed to do?" Dale asked.

"Wait," Charles said. "You're supposed to wait."

"While you do what?" Conlin asked.

"I'm going in to meet the Gunsmith."

"You gonna kill him?" Dale asked.

"Not today," Charles said. "First I've got to take his measure."

"That sounds like engineer talk," Conlin said.

Charles nodded and said, "It is."

Clint was halfway through his beer when the houseman, Hector, reappeared.

"What is it, Hector?" Henry Frick asked.

As Clint watched, the ears of the other four men all seemed to perk up.

"There is a gentleman here to see Mr. Lawrence, sir," the houseman said.

"Who is it?" Frick asked.

"I'll see hi—" Lawrence started, rising, but Frick spoke up again.

"Who is it, Hector?"

"It's Mr. Charles, sir."

"The engineer," Frick said, looking at Clint.

"I'll come out and talk to hi—" Lawrence started, but he was cut off again.

"Bring him in, Hector," Upton said. "We might as well all hear what he has to say."

Lawrence sat back down and said, "Sure." To Clint's mind, he looked very uncomfortable at the prospect.

Hector looked to Frick for the final word, and the man simply nodded.

"This should be very interesting," Henry Frick said to Clint.

"I agree," Clint said.

THIRTY-TWO

Dashmore Charles entered the room and immediately picked out Clint Adams. His heart began to beat faster.

"Mr. Charles," Henry Frick said, rising.

"Mr. Frick," Charles said. They shook hands. "I'm here to make my report to Mr. Lawrence."

"I can take Mr. Charles into another room—" Lawrence started, but for the third time Frick interrupted him. Clint had the feeling he was in the middle of a power struggle. Lawrence, the younger man, might have been trying to wrest power from Frick and the others, who were older.

"Mr. Charles can make his report right here, Evan," Frick said to Lawrence. "The rest of us are very interested."

"But I'm the one who's responsible," Lawrence said. "I hired him."

"Noted, Evan," Frick said. "Mr. Charles, we are all ears."

But Charles didn't respond immediately. He looked at Clint.

"And who's this?" he asked.

"This is Clint Adams," Frick said. "Mr. Adams, this is

Dashmore Charles, our engineer. It is his job to keep us apprised of the structural integrity of our dam."

"I see."

"The Gunsmith, huh?"

Charles, who had a gun on his hip, paid special attention to the one Clint was wearing.

"Mr. Charles," Frick said impatiently, "your report. I believe we have been waiting for this?"

"Yes," the engineer said, "you have."

"Then—"

"Maybe Mr. Charles would like a drink," Lawrence said. "A brandy? Or a beer?"

"A cold beer would be good," Charles said. "It was a long ride."

As if on cue, the waiter, Walter, entered the room.

"Walter," said Lawrence, "please bring Mr. Charles a cold beer."

"Yessir."

"And bring Mr. Adams another."

"Yessir."

He left the room.

"Have a seat, Mr. Charles," Frick said, "and let us have your report."

Charles sat down and began talking about the dam . . .

Clint was not an engineer, but he knew the man was lying.

"So you're saying that there are sections of the dam that need repairs, but that there's no imminent danger," Frick said when Charles was done.

"That's right."

Frick looked at Lawrence.

"The repairs that need to be done," Lawrence asked, "will they be expensive?"

"No." Charles sipped at his beer. His eyes flicked to Clint, then away.

"How soon can you begin?"

"I'll have to make a list of the supplies I'll need," Charles said. "And I'll need some money to purchase them."

Henry Frick sat back in his chair and looked at Evan Lawrence.

"All right, Evan," Frick said, "I suppose that's something you and Mr. Charles can discuss elsewhere."

Lawrence looked like a man who had just been freed from prison. He almost leaped from his seat.

"All right," he said. "We might as well go and look into it, Dash."

"Hmm?" Charles looked surprised. "We're done here?"

"Yes," Lawrence said, "we're done . . . here."

"Can I take my beer with me?"

"Yes."

Charles nodded, and stood up. He took a moment to look directly at Clint, who also stood.

"It was a pleasure to meet you, Adams," Charles said. "I hope we see each other again . . . soon."

Clint couldn't think of any reason why he might want to see Dash Charles again.

After they left the lounge, Evan Lawrence pulled Dash Charles into another, smaller room and slammed the door.

"What the hell are you doing?" he demanded.

"I told you I was going to come up here."

"Yes, but you didn't tell me you were going to come . . . barging in! I didn't want you giving your report in front of other members."

"Well," Charles said, "it's not like I gave the real report."

"What? You lied about the repairs?"

"I don't know if they can be done so cheaply," Charles said. "I mean, we can try, but . . ."

"But what?"

"Never mind," Charles said. "I'll deal with it. That's what you're payin' me for."

"That's right," Lawrence said, "it is."

"So that was the Gunsmith, huh?"

"What? Oh, Adams? Yes, yes, that was him."

"And is he a new member?"

"We won't know that for sure until tomorrow," Lawrence said, "but it looks like Frick is going to succeed in ramming him down the other club members' throats."

"He doesn't look like much, does he?"

"What? I don't know. What's a gunman supposed to look like?"

Charles finished beer and set the mug aside on a nearby table. Lawrence didn't like the faraway look that had come into his eyes.

"You're not going to try anything on club grounds, are you?"

"I'm gonna do my job," Charles said. "Isn't that what you want me to do?"

"Yes!" Lawrence said. "It is! I want you to do your job . . . and nothing else."

Charles's eyes came into focus and he looked at his employer.

"Let's talk about the money for those repairs, huh?" he said.

THIRTY-THREE

"I understand you enjoy a game of poker," Frederick Upton said to Clint.

They had all retaken their seats as Evan Lawrence and Dash Charles left the room.

"Poker?" Clint asked. "I've been known to play a game or two."

"We have a friendly game here every so often," Old Man Foster said.

"Friendly?"

"You know," Bledsoe said, "low stakes."

Clint wondered what "low stakes" meant to these men.

"Perhaps," Upton said, "we can even get a game together tonight."

"That would be interesting," Clint said.

"Gents," the sour-looking Foster said, "why don't we see what we can do to entertain our guest tonight?"

"A guest tonight," Henry Frick pointed out, "but a member tomorrow."

"Yes," Foster said, "indeed."

"Why don't Cole and I see to that," William Bledsoe said.

"Huh?" Cole Foster said.

"Come on, old codger," Bledsoe said, standing up, "we're going to see if we can put together a poker game."

"Poker!" Foster said. "Good." He staggered to his feet and followed Bledsoe from the room with a painfully slow gait.

That left Clint in the room with Frick and Upton.

"Do you want another beer?" Upton asked.

"No, thanks."

"What would you like to do now?" Frick asked.

"Actually," Clint said, "I'd like to go to my room, freshen up a bit, get myself into shape if there's going to be a late-night poker game."

"You can do that," Frick said. "We can have someone come up and tell you if there's going to be a game, and when."

"That'd be fine," Clint said. "I've also got a book I've been trying to finish."

"I'll see what's going on with Evan and the engineer," Upton said. "See you both later."

Upton left the room.

"About that," Frick said. "The, uh, books. I didn't mean to be so surprised before, when you mentioned it."

"That's okay," Clint said. "You didn't expect that someone with my reputation would be a reader."

"I didn't expect to hear that my driver was a reader either," Frick said. "I was more amazed at that."

"Why?" Clint asked. "He seems like an intelligent fellow."

"I suppose I never paid that much attention," Frick said. "I mean Hector . . . Walter . . . I don't know how intelligent they are or not. I just don't . . . pay that much attention to the help."

"Well," Clint said, "you're a rich man, after all. You have people . . . working for you . . ."

"I'm a snob," Frick said. "Is that what you mean?"

"I'm just saying," Clint replied, "that wealthy people with servants have a certain . . . attitude toward them." Clint leaned forward. "Henry, you even have an attitude about me."

"You?" Frick said. "I'm putting you forward for membership in this club."

"Yes," Clint said, "because of my reputation, not because of who I am."

Frick sat back thoughtfully.

"Sonofabitch," he said. "I *am* a snob."

Clint laughed.

"You mean that never occurred to you, ever?" Clint asked him.

Frick shook his head. From the look on his face, Clint thought the man was telling the truth.

THIRTY-FOUR

"Raise."

Clint looked across the poker table at Frederick Upton. He felt sure that Upton thought he had tricked Clint into this game. Actually, after Clint told Henry Frick that he was a snob, and Frick agreed, the two men sort of bonded over that, and Frick offered to bankroll him in the game.

"Why would you do that?" Clint asked.

"Because they think they're bamboozling you into this game," Frick said. "I don't play. But I'd like to help you take their money."

"In that case," Clint said, "I accept."

The buy-in was fifty thousand, and nobody questioned where Clint Adams had come up with that amount—in cash.

They had been playing for two hours, and Clint's luck was going bad. Half of his buy-in was now sitting in front of Frederick Upton, who turned out to be a pretty damn good poker player.

The other players were Bledsoe and Evan Lawrence, as well as two members Clint had not met before, Andrew Chelton and Blake Green.

Chelton had opened the first round of five-card draw with a thousand-dollar minimum, but Upton had immediately said, "Raise," and tossed an extra five thousand into the pot.

Bledsoe, Lawrence, and Green called, and the play came to Clint, who was seated right across from Upton. Clint had the feeling that at least two of the players were in collusion with Upton to take his money. In a saloon he might have called them on it. Here he decided just to go with it.

"Call," he said.

"Cards?" Chelton, the dealer, asked.

Bledsoe and Lawrence took three, Green one, and Chelton three.

Upton stood pat.

"I'll play these," Clint said.

Everyone was surprised that there were two pat hands in one round.

Chelton had opened, so he said, "Check."

"Ten thousand," Upton said.

Bledsoe and Lawrence folded. Green called. The play came around to Clint.

"Call," he said, "and raise." He pushed the rest of his money into the pot.

"All in, eh?" Upton asked.

"Why not?"

"Well," Upton said, "I could make it difficult for you and raise, but instead I'll just call."

Green folded.

"Mr. Adams?" Chelton said. "Your hand, please?"

Clint tossed two kings on the table.

"You stood pat with two kings?" Chelton asked.

Watching from the sidelines, Henry Frick put his hand over his face.

"Frederick?" Chelton asked.

Upton looked across the table at Clint, then tossed his cards on the table.

"Two queens?" Chelton said.

Upton shrugged and said, "Your hand, Adams."

Frick's mouth hung open as Clint raked in his pot.

He was now ahead.

They took a break after five hours. It was the middle of the night. Two players, Green and Chelton, had dropped out. Clint thought they were the two Upton was working with.

"How much do you have?" Frick asked.

"Almost two hundred thousand," Clint said.

"Shouldn't you quit?" the man asked nervously.

"Not until the game is over, Henry."

"And who decides when the game is over?" Frick asked.

"The last man standing."

A small bar had been set up for the players, who were imbibing during the break—all except Clint. He did not drink while he was playing poker, not even during a break.

"Gentlemen?" Upton said. "Back to the table?"

"Let's go," Clint said.

The four men went back to the table.

At the back of the house at that moment, Dash Charles was opening a door and admitting both Dale and Conlin.

"What's goin' on?" Conlin asked. "We been waitin' out there for hours."

"I wanted to make sure we weren't seen," Charles said. "Some of the members are playing poker with Adams upstairs."

"What are you doin'?" Dale asked.

"They gave me a room."

"And what about us?" Dale asked.

"Camp out, but stay close," Charles said. "I'll call you when I need you."

"Camp out?" Conlin asked.

"We're hungry!" Dale complained.

"Relax," Charles said.

He reached down to the floor and came up with a basket he had stocked from the kitchen.

"I don't think they'll miss some cold chicken," he said. "Now go."

"We need something to drink," Conlin declared.

"There's also a bottle of whiskey in there," Dash Charles said. "Don't drink it all!"

"But—but—" Conlin said, but Charles closed the door in their faces.

Henry Frick watched the game unfold from the sidelines, but he could see what was happening. He knew Upton would have somebody working with him, but he wanted to back Clint Adams, and it had turned out to be the right thing to do. Upton was now alone at the table, without his cohorts, and Frick watched with pleasure as all the money on the table started to flow Clint Adams's way.

And when the game was finally over, the last man standing was, indeed, Clint Adams.

THIRTY-FIVE

Clint awoke the next morning with a carpetbag full of cash in his room. Six men, fifty thousand, a total of three hundred thousand. He repaid Henry Frick the fifty thousand he'd backed him with, and split the rest with him. He had not expected to come out of this with a hundred and twenty-five thousand dollars.

Now he had to go down for breakfast with the club members, and leave the money in the room. He wasn't comfortable with that, considering the fact that Frederick Upton had tried to double whipsaw him. Who said he wouldn't break into his room to get his money back?

There was a knock on his door before he could make a decision. When he opened it, Henry Frick was standing there.

"Good morning," Clint said. He backed up to let Frick enter. The man was carrying a bag, the kind banks used for money.

"I thought you might need some help," Frick said.

"With the money?"

Frick nodded.

"Would you like me to put it in the safe for you?"

"Who has the combination to the safe?"

"The club treasurer."

"And who's that?"

"Me."

"In that case . . ."

Clint walked to the bed, opened the bag. Frick approached and Clint transferred the money to the bag he was holding.

"You taught Fred Upton a lesson in poker," Frick said. "I wouldn't put it past him to try and get his money back."

"Is that how members treat each other in this club?" Clint asked.

"You're not a member yet," Frick said. "Not until this morning's meeting."

"Okay."

"You want to come with me while I put this in the safe?" Frick asked. "Then we can go and have breakfast."

"Sure," Clint said. "Lead the way."

When they stepped out into the hall, Clint saw that Jason was there.

"Just to be safe," Frick said.

"Morning, Jason."

"Good morning, sir."

Frick and Jason led Clint downstairs to an office, where Frick put the money bag into a Mosler Safe.

"Now let's have that breakfast," Frick said.

"Jason, too?"

"I'll eat in the kitchen, Mr. Adams," Jason said. "Don't worry about me."

Clint looked at Frick, who shrugged.

"You can't cure all the snobbery in one day."

Jason went to the kitchen while Frick took Clint to the main dining room.

"There's the big winner!" Frederick Upton called out. "Come on, sit down and enjoy a hearty breakfast."

Clint looked around the table. All the poker players were there, as well as Cole Foster. No one else. He wondered where all the other rich club members were.

"Is this everybody?" he asked Frick.

"At the moment," Frick said. "Come on, sit down."

Clint and Frick took the empty chairs at the table, sitting next to each other. The table was covered with platters of food—eggs, bacon, ham, potatoes, biscuits, flapjacks. Everything a man could want—well, almost.

"No steak?" Clint asked.

"We can get you some," Frick said.

"No," Clint said. "This will do."

"Then dig in."

THIRTY-SIX

The meeting to consider Clint's membership was to take place after breakfast. During breakfast the talk was about politics and business. Clint just sat back and listened. He didn't hear anything he thought Jeremy Pike would be interested in. More and more he was thinking that Pike's concern was going to end up being the dam.

After breakfast, Frick put his hand on Clint's shoulder.

"Take a walk around the grounds," he said. "When the meeting is over, I'll come and find you."

"Okay."

The members got up and filed out, laughing, slapping each other on the back. Apparently, at breakfast, they had solved the county's financial problems.

The cook, a black woman named Pandora, came out of the kitchen and asked Clint, "More coffee?"

"That would be nice."

She collected a bunch of plates, carried them into the kitchen, and came back with a coffeepot. She filled his cup, left the pot, and carried some more dishes back to the kitchen.

When she came back out, Clint asked, "Need some help?"

She looked him up and down. In her thirties, she was what most people would call a handsome woman.

"This ain't men's work."

"I don't mind giving you a hand."

She looked him up and down again and said, "I don't mind if I let you."

Together they finished cleaning off the table and carrying everything to the kitchen.

"Just put 'em on the table," she said, "less'n you wanna help me wash 'em."

"That ain't men's work," he said, grinning.

She grinned back, revealing even, white teeth. The smile changed her from handsome to pretty. She was a sturdily built woman wearing a simple cotton dress. Her hair was cut short. Take her out of the kitchen, put her in a better dress, and she'd become beautiful. Her skin was like chocolate, and smooth as silk.

She turned to the sink and started washing dishes. Clint went and got his coffee cup, then came back into the kitchen.

"How do you like working here, Pandora?"

"I like it fine."

"Seems to me somebody who cooks as well as you could run her own restaurant."

"You got some money you wanna invest?"

"I might."

She turned her head and looked at him over her shoulder.

"You serious?"

"Would it be a problem for you to leave here?"

"No problem."

"Would it be a problem for you to talk about what you've seen and heard up here?"

"What you think I seen and heard?"

"I don't know," he said. "What goes on up here?"

"Nothin' much," she said. "Men playin' boys' games."

"High finance?"

"Don't know nuthin' 'bout that," she said.

"What do you know about?"

"My kitchen."

"What happens in the kitchen?"

She looked at him over her shoulder again.

"I cooks, and I cleans," she said.

"And?"

"Usually that's it. But not last night."

"What happened last night?"

"I cooked, but the food disappeared."

"Disappeared?"

"At night."

"Somebody with a late-night appetite?"

"Gotta be a couple o' somebodies," she said.

"Did it ever happen before?"

She shook her head.

"Just last night."

"So it's odd."

She nodded. "Yeah, it's odd."

"What went missing?"

"A mess of fried chicken," she said, "and a bottle of whiskey."

"Only last night."

"Yep."

"How many strangers are in the house?"

"Two," she said.

"Me."

"You, and that engineer fella."

"Maybe he got hungry during the night."

"Maybe," she said, "but there was one other thing."

"What's that?"

"Back door was unlocked."

"That unusual?"

"Real unusual," she said. "I makes sure it's locked every night 'fore I go to bed."

"You have a room in the house?"

"I do," she said. She looked over her shoulder again, gave him a mischievous look full of promise. "You wanna know where it is?"

He smiled.

"Desperately."

THIRTY-SEVEN

After his conversation with Pandora—a very promising conversation—he went out the back door and did what Frick suggested. Took a walk around the grounds. About a hundred yards from the house he found a bunch of chicken bones. They had been picked clean, first by men, then by animals. He didn't find a whiskey bottle, but he did find the cap of one.

Looked to him like the engineer, Dash Charles, had had some help.

He went back into the house.

He found a room with a pool table, picked out a cue, and started to shoot balls. No game, just random balls. After about fifteen minutes the engineer appeared at the door.

"You shoot?" Clint asked.

"Some."

"Grab a cue."

Charles entered the room and picked a pool cue off the wall. Clint racked the balls.

"You break," he said.

"Thanks."

Both men were wearing their guns, but that certain tension was not in the air. Clint could always feel it when a man was close to drawing his gun, and Charles wasn't.

Not yet.

They started shooting a simple game of pool, not much in the way of conversation going on. Charles was the first to talk while Clint was shooting.

"Heard you had an interesting night."

"It was all right."

"Upton always did fancy himself a poker shark," Charles said. "I guess you proved he wasn't."

"Maybe I just got lucky."

"Not when you took him and his boys."

"Well now," Clint said, "*they* weren't very good players."

Clint shot five balls in a row before he missed. He stepped aside.

"How are you doing on your problem?" he asked as Charles bent over the table.

"What problem is that?"

"The dam," Clint said. "It's in need of repairs, isn't it?"

Charles stood up straight without shooting a ball and looked at Clint.

"You an engineer?"

"No," Clint said, "just somebody who can tell when a wall is going to fall down."

"You're wrong." Charles bent over the table and took a shot. "It just needs some shorin' up in places."

"Is that what's in your report?"

The man stood up again. Suddenly there was tension in the air after all.

"Look, Adams," Charles said, "you'd be smart to stay out of my business."

"This is my business," Clint said, "or it will be once they make me a member of the club."

That made Charles laugh.

"You think that's what they're talkin' about in their meeting?" he asked. "Makin' you a member?"

"Among other things."

Charles shook his head, leaned over, and took a shot, then stood up again.

"You're in for a surprise, my friend," he said. He went over to the wall rack and returned the pool cue, then walked to the doorway. He turned and looked at Clint and said, before leaving, "A great big surprise."

Clint frowned.

He didn't like surprises.

THIRTY-EIGHT

Clint found his way to Pandora's room and knocked on the door. When she answered and saw it was him, she leaned against the door and said, "Already?"

"Didn't you say you'd be coming back here after you finished the dishes?"

"Well, yeah, darlin'," she said, "but I thought I'd have time to take a bath."

"I couldn't wait," he said, pushing into the room, "and you don't need a bath."

She backed up and he closed the door behind him. She put her fingers inside the collar of her dress and ran them back and forth over her skin.

"Was we talkin' 'bout the same thing in the kitchen?" she asked.

"I thought we were," he said.

She stared at him and started working on the buttons on the front of her dress. As she peeled it off her shoulders, large, bottom-heavy breasts came into view, with big, very dark nipples.

She had wide hips, had to lean over to shove the dress down and shimmy out of it. When she straightened up, he caught his breath. If ever a woman was built for bed, and sex, Pandora was the one.

He moved closer to her, softly cupped her full breasts in his palms, lifting them. He touched the nipples with his thumbs, and she closed her eyes and moaned.

"When I saw you," she said, "I thought we was just gonna use the kitchen floor."

"Too much chance of being interrupted," he said.

"Ain't they's gonna be lookin' for you?"

"Let them look," he said.

He lifted her breasts higher, leaned over, and touched the nipples with his tongue, and then his lips, tugging on them until they were fully distended.

She wasn't very tall, but certainly not short, about five four or so. He slid his hands behind her and cupped her smooth ass cheeks, lifting her. She came up into his arms, wrapped her powerful legs around him. He could feel the muscles in her ass beneath his hands as he carried her to the bed, his face buried in her neck. Her skin was smooth and fragrant with her natural musk, as well as the smell from the kitchen. Clint had been with women before who spent a lot of time in kitchens, and never minded the mix of scents. That was why he told Pandora she didn't need a bath. He loved the way a woman smelled naturally.

He deposited her on the bed, which was barely large enough for the two of them. She immediately got to her knees and began pulling at his clothes. While she unbuttoned his shirt, he unbuckled his gun belt and hung it on her bedpost. His gun had hung on many bedposts over the years, always within easy reach whenever he was sleeping or entertaining a woman.

She pulled his shirt off and went to work on his belt. Before long he was sitting on the bed, trying to pull his boots off while she was groping for his hard cock.

"You don't know what it's like to be cooped up all day wit' deez ol' geezers," she told him. "A gal ain't got no choice but ta play wit' her own self."

He was kind of curious as to what that would have been like to watch, but she was so close, and so warm and so naked, that he couldn't keep his hands off her.

He pulled her to him and kissed her while she grasped his cock with one hand and began to stroke it.

"Oh yeah," she said huskily as he grew harder in her hand, "dat's de way."

Suddenly, she fell onto his lap, engulfing his hard penis with her hot, wet mouth. As she sucked him, she moaned and he sat back on the bed, leaning his weight on his hands and giving himself up to the suction of her mouth . . .

Meanwhile, down in the meeting of the members, Henry Frick was arguing.

"I'm against it," he said.

"Now, wait a minute, Henry," Evan Lawrence said. "You're the one who brought him up here in the first place."

"I know, but—"

"You knew what we were looking for," Lawrence said.

"Yes, but—"

"You can't change your mind on us now, Henry," Fred Upton said. "The matter has been settled."

"Look," Frick said, "this was all before I got to know the man—"

"Yes," Upton said, "and I got to know him last night,

too. And it was an expensive lesson—one I'm looking to return."

"Come on, Henry," Old Man Foster said, "you know this is called a hunting club."

Frick looked at Foster. The man could barely walk, yet somehow he still managed to hunt. Many of the heads mounted on the club walls had been brought in by him.

"Gentlemen," Frick said, "I implore you—"

"Henry," William Bledsoe said, "the vote has been taken."

"The die has been cast," Foster said.

"There's no going back now," Lawrence said.

"For any of us," Fred Upton said.

The other members of his inner circle stared at Henry Frick until he subsided, no longer offering his objections.

"There," said the chairman of the group, Evan Lawrence, "it's settled." He banged his gavel. "The meeting is adjourned. Henry, let's find Mr. Adams."

When Clint couldn't take it anymore, he wrangled the voracious woman off his cock and pushed her down onto her back. He held her arms down as he attacked her breasts with his mouth, then kissed and licked his way down until his face was nestled in that fragrant, if somewhat scratchy, pubic patch. But the hair softened as he wet it with his tongue, and before long the fragrant nectar from her pussy was running over his face, sweet as honey and almost as sticky.

"Ooh, God, you got a tongue on you . . ." she said, cupping his head in her hands. "Oh Lord, you gon' make me scream."

"Don't do that," he said, lifting his head for a moment, "you'll bring the whole house down on us."

She laughed and turned her head into the pillow, so that when she did finally scream—her body wracked by spasms of pleasure she couldn't believe—her screams were muffled . . .

THIRTY-NINE

Afterward, Pandora made her way back to the kitchen, and Clint once again took a walk around the grounds. That was what he was doing when Henry Frick found him.

"There you are," Frick said.

"The meeting over?" Clint asked.

"It is, indeed," Frick said.

"Am I a member?"

Oddly, Frick hesitated a moment, then said, "You are, indeed. Congratulations."

The two men shook hands.

"Is there some sort of induction ceremony?" Clint asked.

"There will be a dinner tonight in your honor," Frick said. "All of the members who are on the grounds will be in attendance."

"Good," Clint said, "I like your cook's, uh, food."

"Yes, Pandora is a wonderful cook," Frick said. "I will instruct her to go all out on your behalf this evening."

"I'm sure it's very special," Clint said, "when she goes all out."

*   *   *

Inside the house Evan Lawrence found Dash Charles and took him into one of the lounges. When they were each seated with brandy snifters in their hands, he spoke.

"The vote went through this afternoon."

"On Adams?"

"That's right."

Charles frowned.

"I'm not sure I'm happy with that."

"Well, you know, Dash," Lawrence said, "it doesn't really matter, since you are not a member of the club."

"I had plans for Adams."

"Change them."

"Don't know if I can."

"My plans for you involve the dam," Lawrence said, "nothing more. You have the bank draft you need to purchase your supplies."

"I do," Charles said, touching his pocket.

"And to hire the men you need to do the job," Lawrence went on.

"Yes," Charles said.

"Then that's the only thing you should be thinking about."

"You're right," Charles said, "it should be the only thing I'm thinking about—but it's not."

"You're going to have to come to terms with it," Lawrence said. "I'm out on a limb for you with this dam."

"Don't worry about the dam, Evan," Charles said. "It'll be taken care of."

"It better be," Lawrence said. "Don't let me down."

Frick and Clint continued to walk. They got around to the back of the house, and Clint kept Frick away from the place where he'd found the chicken bones.

"That's our preserve back there," Frick said with a wave of his arm. "Our members are always hunting."

"I haven't heard any shooting since I've been here," Clint commented.

"That's because no one's been out while you've been here," Frick said. "But I think they might like to take you out with them."

"I told you," Clint said, "I don't hunt and kill for sport."

"I understand that," Frick said, "but now you are a member of the South Fork Fishing and Hunting Club."

"That's true."

"Whatever you shoot," Frick said, "we can give to Pandora to cook, rather than mount it."

Clint nodded, still not sure he wanted to take part in such a hunt, but maybe he wouldn't have to. He was now a member, and he'd found somebody on the inside who might talk to Jeremy Pike and tell him what he wanted to know. The only thing was, he didn't know how to get a message to Pike from here.

He just hoped that Pike got the message he'd sent over to Solomon's from his hotel.

Henry Frick left Clint alone behind the house and went back inside. He was not happy at all with the way things had gone since bringing Clint Adams to the club. He found he liked the man much more than he ever thought he would.

He went to the kitchen and told Pandora that that night's dinner needed to be special.

"It's in honor of our new member, Clint Adams."

"I understand, sir," Pandora said. "I'll do my best."

Frick thought the cook looked different, but he couldn't put his finger on what it was exactly.

"Thank you," he said, and left the kitchen.

In the dining room he came up short when he saw Dash Charles standing there, apparently waiting for him.

"Mr. Frick," Charles said to him, "I think we should have a talk."

FORTY

Pandora succeeded in outdoing herself with the dinner, which included both beef and poultry. The table was covered with food, and the members in attendance were Henry Frick and his inner circle, as well as the other poker players.

But Clint was sensing something in the air that he hadn't felt before. It might have been coming from Upton, who was still sore from having lost at the poker game. Or it might have been coming from some of the other members. Maybe they had been outvoted in that morning's meeting.

Clint was seated next to Frick, and across from Upton, who—as it turned out—was the one to extend the invitation to hunt.

"That is what this club is all about," he told Clint. "We are a hunting club."

"I understand that."

"Then we'd like you to come out with us tomorrow morning," Upton said.

Clint looked around the table, saw all the members looking at him expectantly.

"I'd be honored to hunt with you," he said.

There was a "hear, hear" from the entire table, but Clint looked over at the kitchen door and saw Pandora watching him, looking very unhappy.

Later Clint was in one of the lounges with Frick, Upton, and Lawrence. They all had brandy and cigars, and Upton had told him they wanted to discuss the hunting.

"Henry," Upton said, though, before starting, "maybe you should leave this to Evan and me."

"But—"

"After all," Lawrence chimed in, "you don't hunt. You won't be there tomorrow."

Frick looked like he wanted to argue, but in the end, he turned to Clint and said, "I'll say good night, then," and left the room.

"Was that necessary?" Clint asked.

"Henry brought you in, Clint," Upton said, "but in reality, he's on the way out." Clint looked at Lawrence.

"It's true," the younger man said. "There is new thinking coming into play, and Henry is part of the old regime."

"But isn't he friends with Carnegie?" Clint asked. "And isn't Carnegie—"

"Dale Carnegie is behind the new thinking," Upton said, "and he's made it clear that Henry Frick is not part of it."

"I see."

"Now why don't we sit and go over what's going to happen tomorrow?"

Clint nodded, even though he had no desire to go hunting with these two, or anyone.

About an hour after he'd turned in, he heard a light knock on his door. He got up, grabbed his gun, and padded barefoot to the door, wearing only his skivvies. He half expected to see Pandora there, so he was totally surprised to see Jeremy Pike in the hall.

"Let me in, quick," Pike said, "before somebody sees me."

Clint backed away, allowing Pike to enter, then closed the door and turned to face his friend.

"What are you doing here?" Clint asked.

"I got your message," Pike said. "Thought this was the only way we could talk."

Pike walked to the bed and sat down. He was wearing a dark shirt and trousers, a jacket with a gun in a shoulder rig.

"What's happened so far?"

"I've been approved as a member," Clint said, "and they want me to go on a hunt with them tomorrow."

"That's good!"

"Look," Clint said, "I think your concern should be the dam, after all." He sat down on the other side of the bed. "I talked with Charles, the engineer. I think he's going to suggest a cheap way to fix it."

"There's nothing else?" Pike asked. "You haven't heard anything else that the government might be interested in?"

"You're talking about political things?" Clint asked. "Or something financial? I might have somebody you could talk to who's heard more than I have."

"Who?"

He told him about Pandora, the cook. Not that they'd slept together, just that she was on the inside, cooked, and served all the meals. And could have heard a lot of things said at the table.

"She'd be great," Pike said. "What does she want?"

"I think," Clint said, "you could get what you want just by setting her up in her own restaurant."

"I'd have to sell that idea to my bosses," Pike said.

"Then sell it," Clint said.

"Okay, look," Pike said, "I'll find out if I can do that and get back to you. Meanwhile, you better just do what you have to do to stay here."

"You mean hunt?"

"Yeah," Pike said, "I mean hunt. Look, if I get this okayed for the girl, this'll be the last thing I ask of you."

Clint frowned, looked down at the gun in his hand.

"Will you do it?"

"I'll do it," Clint said. "Yeah, I'll do it."

"Thanks, Clint."

Pike got up and went to the door.

"I'll get back to you as soon as I can."

"Okay."

"Take care of yourself," Pike said, "and take good care of that girl."

"I will," Clint promised.

Pike slipped from the room into the hall, and was gone. Clint went to the front window, but didn't see any sign of the Secret Service man leaving. He might have gone out the back way.

He slid his gun back into the hanging holster and sat on the bed. If Pike could get through to his boss in one day, this could all be over by tomorrow. He was anxious to be gone from Pittsburgh—and South Fork—heading back to the West, but he wasn't sure he could leave without making sure that the dam was going to receive the proper treatment.

He still thought it was about the dam.

FORTY-ONE

In the morning he rose early and went down to the dining room for breakfast. The men were all there, dressed for hunting. Only Henry Frick was missing.

"Where's Henry?" he asked.

"He had to go back to Pittsburgh," Upton said.

"Jason drive him?"

"Yes."

"Will he be back?"

"Yes, tonight," Lawrence said.

"After the hunt," Upton said.

"What are we hunting for exactly?" Clint asked.

"We have a wild boar out there," Upton said. "We brought some over from Africa. This is the last one—and the biggest. We've been meaning to have a try at him."

"He'd make good eating if you could bag him," Lawrence said to Clint.

"Especially with Pandy doing the cooking," Old Man Foster said.

Clint was surprised that the older man was also dressed for hunting.

"So we're all going?" Clint asked.

"Yes," Upton said, "all of us."

Upton saw Clint looking at Foster.

"Foster's the most accomplished hunter among us," he told Clint.

"Even if he is a little past it," Lawrence said, keeping his voice low.

Since Clint had been the last one down to breakfast, he was the last one to finish eating.

"When you're done," Upton told him, "grab your rifle and meet us out back."

"Will I need my horse?"

"No," Upton said, "we hunt on foot."

"Okay," Clint said, "I'll meet you there."

While he finished eating, Upton and Lawrence loitered at the entryway to the dining room. Pandora came out, leaned over Clint so she could pour him some more coffee. She looked over her shoulder, saw that Upton and Lawrence were still there.

"You gotta be careful out there," she whispered to Clint.

Clint didn't flinch. She was keeping her voice down for a reason.

"Careful of what?"

"Not what," she said. "Who. Them."

"Come on, Adams," Upton shouted. "Finish that coffee and let's get going!"

Pandora straightened up abruptly and hurried back to the kitchen.

What was that warning about? he wondered.

He went to his room to retrieve his rifle and pistol, then hurried around to the back of the house. The hunters were gathered there, holding their rifles and shotguns. Upton,

Lawrence, Bledsoe, Foster, and the two poker players, Green and Chelton, were all present.

"Are we going in a group?" Clint asked.

"Well, we are," Upton said. "We usually hunt in groups of threes."

"That leaves me the odd man out," Clint said.

"In more ways than one," Upton said, turning his rifle toward Clint.

"What are you doing?"

"Just stand fast," Upton said. "All the guns are pointed at you."

Clint looked around. Sure enough, the barrels of six weapons were all pointing at him.

"Them," Pandora had said.

And she had meant . . . all of them.

FORTY-TWO

"Put your hands up," Upton said.

Clint obeyed. Upton lowered his own rifle, stepped forward, and took Clint's rifle and pistol from him.

"Is this what it's been about all along?" Clint asked. "Getting me out here to hunt me?"

"We've hunted everything else," Upton said. "We've never hunted a legend."

"And the meeting today?" Clint asked. "It wasn't about making me a member."

"It was about making you our quarry," Upton said. "And we voted yes—although the vote was not unanimous."

"Frick."

"Yes."

"Is he all right?" Clint asked. "Have you killed him?"

"Of course not," Lawrence said. "He's a member of our club."

"He really did go to Pittsburgh," Upton said. "He'll stay there until this is over."

"You won't get away with this," Clint said. "There're people who know I'm here."

"It doesn't matter," Upton said. "We'll just tell people it was a hunting accident."

"They won't believe it," Clint said. "Not the people I'm working with."

"What people?" Foster asked.

"The government," Clint said to the older man. "They're very interested in what goes on at this club. They sent me in to find out."

Foster looked at Upton. The other men looked around at each other.

"He's lying," Upton said. "He's trying to save his hide."

"Not my hide," Clint said. "Yours."

"What are you talking about?" Upton asked.

"If you send me out there and then come hunting me," Clint said, "I'll have to kill you." He looked at the others. "All of you."

Upton laughed.

"How do you figure that?" Upton asked. "We know the terrain, you don't. We're armed, you aren't."

"I've killed men before," Clint said, "you haven't. That's the difference."

The other men looked to Upton for guidance.

"No," he said. "We have the advantage." He looked at his friends. "We're not changing our plans. Even if he is working for the government, what do they know? He's here, and he's not going anywhere but out there. Besides that, what does he know? Nothing."

Upton looked at Clint.

"We'll give you a ten-minute start. That's a hundred acres out there. If you make it to the other end, then maybe you'll go free."

"I'll come after you," Clint said.

Upton laughed.

"You won't make it. If we don't get you, there's game out there that will."

"Upton," Clint said, "you can stop this right now."

"See, fellas?" Upton said. "He's scared. The Gunsmith is scared."

"I'm not scared," Clint said. "I feel sorry for you. You don't know what you're doing. And you're getting them into something they can't handle."

"I can handle anything," Old Man Foster said, "with this." He was holding a new side-by-side double-barreled hunting rifle. "Maybe these men don't know what they're doing, but I've hunted all over the world, all kinds of big game. I'm looking forward to this." He jerked the barrels of his rifle. "Get moving, Gunsmith."

Clint looked at the rest of the men.

"You heard the man, Adams," Upton said. "It's time. Your ten minutes start . . . now!"

FORTY-THREE

Clint moved.

He trotted down a path into the preserve, came across what was left of the chicken bones he figured Dash Charles had given to his friends. He moved about twenty yards past that point, farther into the trees, when he heard it.

"Adams."

He turned at the sound of his name. He saw Dash Charles standing there.

"Are you in on this?" Clint asked. The man's gun was in his holster.

"Not me," Charles said. "I do my killing face-to-face, on equal terms."

"Then what are you doing here?"

"I told Frick what they were planning," Charles said, "only he already knew. He didn't know how to help you, though. I told him I did." He took his gun out of his holster. "He told me where they always start their hunts from. I figured I'd wait for you here."

"Where are your friends?" Clint asked. "The ones who ate the chicken you stole?"

"I've got them doing something else, down by the dam."

He reversed the gun in his hand and tossed it to Clint, who caught it deftly. He spun the cylinder to make sure it was loaded. It was the same caliber as his own, so he had plenty of extra shells on his gun belt, which they'd left him with.

"Thanks. And here I thought you were going to give me a try."

"I thought about it," Charles said. "I'd stay and help ya, but I just ain't that helpful."

"This'll do fine," Clint told him.

Charles tossed him a salute and ran off into the brush.

Upton looked at his watch and said, "Okay, let's go."

"It's only been eight minutes," Bledsoe said.

"So what?" Upton asked. "Foster and Green, you're with me. We'll circle to the east. The rest of you circle around to the west."

"He's mine," Foster said. "I'll get him."

"We'll see, old man," Upton said. "We'll see."

They split up, two groups of three.

Clint moved a little farther into the preserve before he decided his best move was to stop and wait. He found a likely spot, where he could sit in some brush out of sight, and hunkered down. Then he heard something farther in the brush behind him, something snorting and rutting. He realized it must be the boar they were talking about.

The big one.

As it moved through the brush, it sounded very big. Clint had seen some wild pigs before, but never a boar.

"What's that?" Green said.

"That's the boar," Upton said. "Coming from over there. Come on."

"We're not after boar," Foster said. "We're after Adams."

"If the boar hears Adams moving around, it'll move toward him. We find the boar, we'll find Adams."

"I get first shot at him," Foster grumbled.

"The first one who sees him gets the first shot," Upton said.

Foster grumbled some more.

The boar sounded like he was getting closer, so Clint started to move again. It soon became apparent to him that the members of the club were not the only ones hunting him.

FORTY-FOUR

Clint finally decided there was no way he could get to the other end of the hundred-acre preserve. His only choice, then, was to circle back. And all the way, he was aware of the snorting, snuffling boar behind him.

"He's circling back," Foster said.

"Are you sure, Cole?" Upton asked.

"The trail is as clear as day, Fred," Foster said.

"Cole, your old eyes—"

"May not be able to read newspaper print so well anymore, you young pup," Foster said, "but I can still read signs better than you ever could!"

Upton shrugged and said, "Okay. What about the wild boar?"

"Right behind him," Foster said. "And closing in."

"Well," Upton said, "I hope we get Adams before the boar gets him."

The other three hunters were finding no sign of Clint Adams.

"Evan," Bledsoe said, "we should turn back. Old Man Foster's probably got the scent by now."

"He's right," Chelton said. "It's no use."

"Damn it!" Lawrence said. "Yeah, yeah, okay, let's turn back."

Clint could see the roof of the house in the distance. If he could make it—but suddenly he heard the boar behind him. The animal broke from the brush and came at him. It was huge, bigger than any pig he'd ever seen. And with those tusks, it would have given a mountain lion a tussle.

He knew if he fired, he'd be giving his position away, but in that split second he also knew he had no choice. He only hoped the pistol was a big enough caliber to do the job. He had no idea how thick the animal's hide was.

He drew the gun—odd in his hand, even if it was the same caliber as his own—and fired twice. Both shots stuck the boar in the head, one right between the eyes. It stumbled, tried to maintain its feet just out of instinct, and then went down in a heap.

Hurriedly, Clint reloaded.

"Where did those shots come from?" Upton asked.

"Back near the house," Foster said.

"If he makes it to the house . . ." Upton said.

"We're not that far behind him," Foster said. "All I need is one clear shot."

Clint reached the remnants of those chicken bones again. There were just enough there to tell him where he was. He figured he'd been running around that preserve for a few hours now. All he had to do was walk up the path to the house.

Foster sighted down the twin barrel of his rifle and said, "I've got him."

"Well," Upton said, "take the shot."

Foster cocked both hammers.

"I don't think so," a voice said from behind them. "Drop the guns, boys."

Foster froze with his finger just off the trigger.

Clint heard them coming and took cover behind a tree. In moments he saw Evan Lawrence, with Bledsoe and Chelton, coming along the path.

He stepped out and said, "Hold it right there."

The three men froze when they saw him.

"Hey," Bledsoe said. "Who gave him a gun? That's not right."

"I found it," Clint said.

"Maybe it doesn't work," Chelton said hopefully.

"You want to find out?" Clint asked.

The three men held their rifles loosely. Clint wondered if they were going to try.

"No," Lawrence said, "no. We don't."

"Drop the guns."

Lawrence dropped his, and Chelton and Bledsoe followed. Suddenly, Upton, Foster, and Green came up the path, with a fourth man walking behind them, holding a gun.

"Found these three wandering around out there," Jeremy Pike said.

"Where the hell did you come from?" Clint asked.

"Tell you later."

"My new rifle is still out there," Foster complained. "It'll get ruined."

"You're not going to need it where you're going," Pike said to the old man.

FORTY-FIVE

"Henry Frick," Pike said.

"How did he find you?" Clint asked.

"He went to your hotel, found out you sent me a message here with the doorman."

"I thought I could trust the doorman," Clint said.

"I think Frick gave him more money than you did."

"Lucky for me," Clint said.

"What are you complaining about?" Jeremy Pike asked. "You bagged a wild boar. In North America yet. Nobody else can say that."

It was two days later. Clint was back in his hotel room, had met with Pike at Solomon's again before leaving Pittsburgh. He'd told Pike everything that had happened at the club, except for his dalliance with Pandora—oh, and the money he'd won playing poker, which he had since put in the bank.

"How are you doing with Pandora?" Clint asked. "Is she going to get her restaurant?"

"She is. She's giving us some real dirt on that bunch," Pike said.

"Political stuff, huh?"

"That's right," Pike said. "And financial. They had some plans for their own private little coup. Just like they had their own little club within a club."

"So the South Fork Fishing and Hunting Club is safe?"

"The other members didn't know a thing about it," Pike said. "So they're free to go on running their club with all their rich members."

"And Frick?"

"He walked," Pike said, "but I hear Dale Carnegie's out for his hide."

"Too bad," Clint said. "I never got a chance to thank him—or Charles."

"The engineer?"

"Yes," Clint said. "I owe him, too. I hope he does his job all right with that dam."

"I'm not so sure he will," Pike said.

"Why?"

"Evan Lawrence was paying him," Pike said. "And Lawrence is going to jail."

"So he'll make a deal with someone else," Clint said. "It's still the club's responsibility."

"More rich men maybe," Pike said, "wanting it done on the cheap?"

"I hope not," Clint said. "If that dam ever went, a lot of people would be in trouble."

AUTHOR'S NOTE

On May 31, 1889, the South Fork Dam failed, causing the Johnstown Flood. Approximately 20 million gallons of water killed 2,209 people, and caused $17 million in damage.

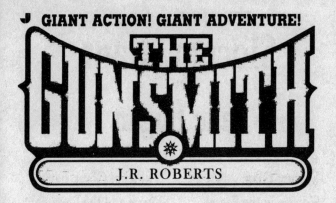

GIANT ACTION! GIANT ADVENTURE!

THE Gunsmith

J.R. ROBERTS

penguin.com/actionwesterns

M455AS0812

DON'T MISS A YEAR OF

Slocum Giant
by
Jake Logan

penguin.com/actionwesterns

M457AS0812

LONGARM

GIANT-SIZED ADVENTURE FROM AVENGING ANGEL LONGARM.

BY TABOR EVANS

penguin.com/actionwesterns

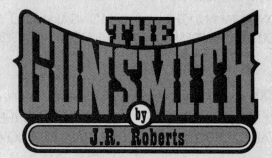